Caleb's Regret
Forever Midnight MC
Book Two

Victoria Gale

Published in 2020 by

Deryn Publishing

United Kingdom

Second Edition

© 2020 Deryn Publishing

All characters, places and events are fictional. Any resemblance to real persons, places or events is purely coincidental.

The moral rights of the author have been asserted.

All rights reserved. No part of this publication may be reproduced, copied, stored or distributed in any form, without prior written permission of the publisher

> *"A friend is someone who walks into a room when everyone else is walking out."*
>
> *– Gary Moore*

PROLOGUE

Amber

I sucked in a lungful of the cold night air and pulled my coat tight at the collar. My head hurt, my feet hurt, and exhaustion threatened to knock me on my ass and keep me there. That's what I got for pulling a double shift at the airport. My third this week.

I rubbed my head and tried to block out the incessant droning of the planes that almost drowned out the ringing of my phone in my bag.

"Hey, Caleb," I said, relief evident in my voice when I answered. It was hard being the girlfriend of a member of the Forever Midnight Motorcycle Club. More so now that Caleb's dad had been killed and he had taken on the mantle of President. "Where are you?" I asked.

"Still in Mexico, baby. We got a lead on the fucker who took dad out and should catch up with him in a day or so. We'll be home straight after that."

I huffed out a breath and rubbed my head again. My headache pounded full force, as did the dread kicking me in the gut. I knew who Caleb was, and I knew neither he nor his brother, Cane, could leave finding the guy who killed their dad to the cops. But that didn't mean I was happy about it, nor that I wasn't afraid of what would happen to him in the process. That worry had been the reason for my double-shift. For all the double-shifts I'd taken since the funeral and Caleb's leaving a week ago. It was easier for me to pass out exhausted than try to fall asleep.

"Is that a plane in the background?" Caleb asked. "You still in fucking work or starting another shift? I told you already, you don't need to do that. I can take care of us. Just quit already. They work you like a dog."

Despite myself, I smiled. We'd had this conversation a thousand times. Just as it was in Caleb's nature to go after the person who killed his dad, it was also in his nature to be a bossy fuck who thought it was his job to take care of my every need. But it was in my nature to work, and he knew it.

"I'll tell you what," I said, deciding to appease him. "I've built up some lieu time. As soon as you get back, I'll cash it in. We can get away for a break together. Lord knows we could both use a vacation."

"You're not wrong there," he said. "But Cane--"

"Cane's a big boy who can take care of himself. Besides, he'll have Bono and the others to look out for him."

"I'm just not sure it's the right time for him to be alone. Dad was the only blood-family we had. You know how fucking broody Cane gets."

I gave a wry laugh. "Don't I just. He's much the same as his brother in that respect. Give him something to focus on and he'll be fine."

"Yeah, and what about me?"

"Well," I said, smiling. "I'll see to making sure you're okay. You know, it's part of my job description as Lounge Manager to ensure everyone gets a five-star service."

"Yeah. What sort of five-star service do you have in mind for me?"

I glanced along the walkway leading from the departure lounge and the short-term parking opposite and towards employee parking, my destination. No one was in sight. "It's a special service I reserve for tattooed muscle-men named Caleb Landon," I said, almost shouting to be heard above the sound of an airplane taxiing on the runway. "The man who makes my core throb and my panties wet just by saying my name."

Caleb growled down the phone. "Now, Amber," he said in a

deep and sultry voice that made me chuckle, "that sure sounds like a service I could get into. Just as long as there's no other fucker named Caleb Landon within an eight-thousand-mile radius of your location."

I laughed again. "I'm pretty sure the diameter of the Earth is a little under eight-thousand miles."

"You're right. It's not fucking far enough. How many miles away is Pluto?"

"I have no idea. We're probably talking in the billions."

I heard a background voice shouting Caleb's name, followed by a commotion. The voices were indistinct, and I couldn't make out what was going on.

After a moment, Caleb returned to our call. "Sorry, babe. I gotta go. I'll be back soon, I promise."

"Okay," I said, my worry flooding back. "Take care of yourself. Come home to me and we'll take that break, okay?"

"Amber. Seriously, I can't leave Cane."

But you can leave me, I resisted mentioning. Instead, I said, "I know, family comes first."

"Jesus. Do we really have to fucking go there now?"

"Go where?" I asked, my tired mind confused by the shift in his tone. "Ah," I said, as realization clicked into place. Family. It always seemed strange to me that Caleb would get pissed off when I noted his family came first, and that included all the brothers of Forever Midnight, especially when it was true.

"Look. I'll call tomorrow and see you in a couple of days. You can fucking lecture me all you want then. I gotta go."

"You can be a complete fucking asshole sometimes, you know that?"

"Yeah, I do. It's why you love me," he said, trying to make his voice light again. "I love you, too, you know?"

"I know. Just hurry home."

With that, he ended the call, and I let out another huffed breath. It was great to hear Caleb's voice, but the worry it would be for the last time filled me with an icy chill that had nothing to do with the weather.

I shook my head and walked towards the lighted parking lot. I noted the battery on my phone was down to five percent and made a mental note to put it on charge in the car before chucking it in my bag and fumbling to find my keys. Caleb had told me to always have them in hand when I approached my car to be sure no one could jump me in the seconds it took to get them out. I always scoffed at the idea. This was an airport for goodness' sake, you couldn't find better security. Still, the night had a hollow feel to it, even with the bustle of the airport behind me. Eerie clouds swirling around the moon like black ink in water. I shivered and increased my pace while reminding myself I'd made this same journey day in and day out, and I was perfectly safe. Maybe knowing I was going home to an empty house with Caleb over a thousand miles away in Mexico had me on edge. Tiredness didn't help.

I zigzagged through the parked cars, desperate to reach the safety of my own and be on the road for my one-hour journey to Castle Rock and home. I told myself it was my imagination when footsteps sounded to my '. After all, who could hear them above the sound of the planes? But then they got faster, and I heard running. I turned around in time to see someone charging at me from a tree by the side of the lot.

My heart thundered. I gripped my car key and pointed it out between my knuckles, ready to use it as a weapon should the need arise.

"Amber," a voice called at the same time as my pursuer's face came into view, highlighted by the LED lot light.

"Damn it, Sophia," I said. "Are you trying to give me a heart attack?"

She linked her arm in mine and pulled me into the open area between the cars. "I just wanted to catch up, is all," she said and shivered. "This place creeps me out after dark."

"So, you decided to creep me out in return," I said.

"Oh, you'll be fine. No one would even think of touching you with that big, bad boyfriend of yours."

"He's not that bad."

"Ooh." Sophia raised an overly plucked eyebrow at me. "That means he is big. Just how big are we talking? Ten? Twelve inches?" I laughed, and she dragged me over to her car. "See you in a few days, chica," she said and hopped in.

I waited until she'd driven off before finding my own car. I chucked my bag on the passenger seat and shrugged off my coat before starting the engine, revving it for a few seconds to kick start the heating. Fastening my seat belt, I turned the radio on at a low volume and headed away from the airport, towards the I-25. I had the next two days off work and planned to spend them huddled in bed with a good book and a hot-water bottle. A bottle of wine wouldn't go amiss either.

I must have been twenty minutes out of Castle Rock when I first heard the rumble of bikes behind me. My first thought was that it was some of the brothers from Forever Midnight, but that notion soon faded when the leading bike came alongside my car and hovered in my blind spot. None of the brothers would pull a stunt like that.

I dropped back a little to let him pass, but he mirrored my actions. Five more bikes joined him, and one pulled up alongside my window, motioning me to pull over.

Yeah, like that was going to happen.

Two of the bikers pulled behind me and turned their lights on high beam. I adjusted my rear-view mirror to avoid their glare and put my foot down on the pedal to pick up speed.

My stomach felt as hard as a rock and my hand shook as I turned off the radio to better focus on my situation. The motorcycles all pulled alongside me, a whirl of noise, leather, and menace. They motioned for me to pull over again. When I didn't, they dropped way back. All bar one, who accelerated well past me before turning in the road and coming back at me in a full-on game of chicken.

"Just run him down," I said, hoping that voicing the words would give me strength. "The damage to him will be far more than it is to you."

My heart pounded and all I could see was the high beam of the bike headed my way. Tears formed in my eyes and I told myself over and over just to head straight, he'd pull out of the way; he had to pull out of the way. But, he didn't.

At the last second, I yanked the steering wheel to the side and the car shot onto the grass verge. I kept my head and control of the vehicle, intent on pulling it back onto the road again, but my wheel struck something, and my tire burst with a loud boom, followed by a whoosh of air, and an incessant flapping. My car slowed instantly and pulled to the left. I had no choice but to ride it out, slow down gradually or risk flipping the car.

As soon as the car stopped, I rushed into my bag and grabbed my phone. Two percent. I almost screamed but tried to make a call anyway. I'd only managed one out of the three numbers I needed to call before it died completely.

My car door yanked open and someone grabbed hold of my arm, leaned across me and unclipped my seatbelt before dragging me out of the car and flinging me against its side.

My heart hammered and my breaths came in shallow gasps as panic and fear swelled inside. I'd been so stupid. I should have kept my foot down. He would have moved.

Five bikes made a circle around me and the man who'd dragged me from my car. In their blinding light, it was hard to see anything other than the smiling face of the dark-haired man before me.

"Amber Gerald, I presume," he said and ran a finger down my cheek. "You hear of the Feral Sons?"

I had. I jerked away and tried to back up a step, but there was nowhere for me to go. "What do you want?" I asked.

He lifted his hand and motioned to the guys on the bikes. To my surprise, they backed away. But when they took up positions around half a mile along either end of the road, I soon realized they were lookouts.

"If you know who I am then you know my boyfriend?" I said, trying to sound braver than I felt.

"Your boyfriend, Caleb Landon, is the reason I'm fucking here. I like to kick a man when he's down, and you're gonna help me do it."

By the dimmed light coming from my car and the moon above, I noted the black spot on his neck was a tattoo of a lion wearing a crown. He saw me staring at it and lifted his chin to give me a better view.

"You like that," he said before running his hand down my cheek, my neck, my chest. "Be sure to tell Caleb exactly what you saw on the guy who hurt you."

I wanted to scream, to lash out. I jerked my knee up, landing a blow to the man's crotch. He stepped back for a moment. I darted away in a run. I hadn't gone three steps when he pushed me to the ground, grabbed my legs, and pulled me closer to him.

"I like a woman with a bit of fight in her," he said as he grabbed my throat.

CHAPTER ONE

(Four Years Later)

Amber

I pulled the car to a stop and turned in my seat to look at my beautiful angel. Her deep brown eyes were so unlike the blue of my own. At least, she had my blonde hair, although I suspected that would change as she got older.

"You ready, Charlie-baby?" I asked. "You excited to see Aunt Sophia, Uncle Franc, and Aunt Caroline?"

She squealed, flapped her legs, and pulled at the straps holding her into her car seat. I wished the nausea rising in my stomach had more to do with excitement than nerves.

Four years. Four years since I'd been south of Denver. It seemed like a lifetime ago. In Charlie's case, it was her lifetime, and then some. Even though I'd never been more than an hour's drive from Castle Rock and the home I once had there, I'd never made the trip, until now.

"Mommy's coming," I said, and got out of the car before opening the back door and freeing Charlie.

"Walk." She wriggled in my arms until I put her down.

"Hold Mommy's hand by the road, Charlie-baby," I said when she tried to run ahead. She stopped in her tracks and waited for me with her hand stretched high ready for me to take hold of it.

My nerves had increased when my surroundings moved away from the big city and into the countryside, and now they felt fit to burst. Still, I wouldn't miss my best friend's wedding for the world. Not after everything she'd done for me.

Before we could reach the door of Sophia's parent's bungalow, where we'd be staying for the next few days, it flew open and she ran out to greet us.

"Hey, chica," she said, pulling me in for a quick hug before crouching to Charlie's level. "Hey, little one, you got a big hug for your Aunt Sophia?" Charlie flung her arms around her neck, and Sophia lifted her from the ground. "Oh, you are getting so big, Charlie. Just make sure you don't get too big too fast or I won't be able to pick you up."

Sophia motioned with her head for us to go inside. "Let me just grab our bags from the trunk first," I said and rubbed my hand over the top of Charlie's head. "Will you be okay with Aunt Sophia for a few seconds?"

"Aunt Sophia," Charlie echoed and clung on tighter to her neck while bouncing up and down.

Sophia laughed. "She'll be fine."

I smiled to myself and returned to the car. Huffing out a deep breath, I took in the views of the town and surrounding countryside. I briefly wondered if we had time to take a hike up to the Castle Rock butte, the namesake of our small town, but decided that Charlie's little legs weren't up to it yet.

Maybe when she's older.

I froze, case in hand, surprised at the thought. Homesickness struck me deep inside. I'd missed this place so much and hadn't even realized it. A knot formed in my throat. This was meant to be a one-time deal. The town held too many bad memories for me to think of coming back again. Although maybe, being home, the good ones would overshadow the bad.

"Amber," Sophia's dad called. Spotting me with the bag, he rushed over and pulled it from my hand. "Come on, let's hurry you inside. I hope you're hungry. Caroline has chili on the stove."

"Thank you, Mr. Cortez."

He shook his head and hefted my bag over his shoulder. "I'm not sure how many times, I've told you to call me Franc."

"Sorry, Franc. Old habits die hard."

As soon as we entered the house, Caroline ran over and fussed over Charlie for a few minutes before turning to me and pulling me in for a hug. "Look at you, as lovely as ever," she said and placed her hand on my cheek. "How are you doing?"

I nodded and smiled. "I'm good. I really am."

"That's great to hear. Wait until you see the fabulous dress Sophia has picked out for you to wear. The little one too. One of her other bridesmaids should be here soon. Sweet girl is pregnant. You know what that's like. Her size is changing daily, so we're doing one final check before the big day to make sure her dress fits." She huffed out an exasperated breath and excused herself to the kitchen and her chili.

"I'll put your bag in the room," Franc called, as Sophia, still carrying Charlie, and I followed Caroline.

"Banana." Charlie squealed and pointed to the fruit bowl on the center island. Sophia sat her on top of the counter and handed her the fruit, peeling it first.

"I'm really glad you could make it," Sophia said reaching over and squeezing my hand.

"Yeah, me too." I wiped a spot of banana from Charlie's face. "I just can't believe you're getting married, and to a man I've only met once. I feel like I'm missing so much of your life."

"I know, chica. Me too." She glanced at Caroline and me and asked us both if it was okay for Caroline to look after Charlie for a few minutes.

"I would love to," Caroline said, turning off the stove and

turning to Charlie. "Would you like to see the big bed where you're staying with Mommy? I got a special teddy just for you to cuddle up with."

"Yay, teddy." Charlie lifted her arms ready to be picked up before Caroline obliged, and they left me and Sophia alone in the kitchen.

"How are you really doing?" she asked.

I sighed. "I'm not gonna lie and say I wasn't as nervous as hell coming, but I'm feeling better already. It's only a few days, and it's not as though I'm going to see anyone besides the guests at the wedding."

A frown deepened on Sophia's brow and she took my hands, leading me to the couch in the living room. "That's what I'm a little worried about," she said, her face going pale as we sat. "I swear, I didn't know until half an hour ago, and it was too late to call you then."

"Know what?" I asked, my palms suddenly sweating.

"Well, you know I mentioned meeting my other bridesmaid a few months ago?"

I did. I'd been glad Sophia had made a new close friend, although a little jealous too. She'd stopped working at the airport not long after I transferred my position to Denver International, and started working as a receptionist at a Doctor's surgery. That's where she'd met Thea. Sophia had said that they'd hit it off straight away, and that as well as being pregnant, Thea had an interest in mental health. I'd also heard a little about her past and it made my own problems seem small in comparison.

"Well," Sophia continued, "in all the times I've met up with Thea, I've never actually seen her boyfriend. I mean, I've spoken to him on the phone and he seems lovely, but I've never met him. She phoned just before you got here. He's worried about her being too... well, pregnant, to drive. You know how some guys get. Way overprotective and all. Although given what Thea's been through, there's no surprise there."

My stomach churned and worry about where this was going had me feeling like I was about to throw up. "You're going a little off track," I said while trying to hold back a burst of hysterical laughter. "What are you trying to tell me? It's not Caleb, is it?" Just saying the words caused a lump in my throat and a knot in my stomach.

"Oh, God, no." Sophia reached over and squeezed my hand. "No. No. It's—"

Before she could say another word, the doorbell rang and I jumped up, unsure whether or not I needed to run and hide.

Franc, oblivious to our conversation, ran in from another room and opened it. "Thea," he said, and pulled a stunning brunette in for a quick hug. When she stepped aside and introduced the man behind her, my breath hitched in my throat.

"I'm so sorry," Sophia whispered and held on to my hand as tight as she could for reassurance. "Maybe he won't even know who you are. It's been a long time and you couldn't have met all the brothers, right?"

"It's a pleasure to meet you," Franc continued. "Don't just stand there. Come in, come in."

Thea entered, and a face I hadn't seen in four years stepped through the door behind her. Sophia clearly had no idea who he was, other than a member of Forever Midnight Motorcycle Club. How could she? We'd been no more than work buddies until that fateful night changed everything. She'd never met Caleb. She'd never met his blood-brother.

Cane froze in the doorway as soon as he spotted me. A deep frown furrowed his brow, and his eyes never left my own. At the edge of my vision, I noted Thea's face fall. Her hand rushed to her belly as she took in the look that must have been on my own face. Following my gaze, she turned to Cane and stepped towards him as though seeking protection. Although, maybe it was reassurance she was after.

"It's good to see you, Cane," I said, managing to find my voice, even though it sounded hollow in my ears.

Franc cleared his throat and, noting the tension, suggested maybe it was best if Cane left.

"No." Sophia stepped between me and the newcomers. "You

can't tell Caleb she's here," she said, rushing to protect me, even though she had no idea who she was speaking to. "You have to promise. She's only here because of me. I won't see her hurt."

Cane looked as though he was about to say something, but Thea brushed her hand along his bearded cheek and turned his head to her. His face softened when he looked at her in a way I never would have thought possible during the time I knew him. It became clear to me then how much Sophia's new friend meant to Cane. It was hard to reconcile the man I knew, the one who liked to screw everything that moved, with the one who looked at Thea as though she was his whole world. Those changes made me wonder how much Caleb had changed too, and whether or not those changes had been for the better or worse.

Cane grabbed Thea's hand and took a step towards me and Sophia. "Thea," he said by way of introduction. "This is Amber. Amber, this is Thea, my fiancé."

"Amber," Thea said as though sounding my name out for the first time. "As in, not just Sophia's Amber, but Caleb's Amber too?"

I smiled wistfully despite myself. "No one's thought of me as Caleb's in a long time."

Thea stepped forward with her hand extended. "I'm sorry," she said. "I've heard a lot about you."

"Not all good, I'm sure." Her face dropped to the floor, and

I had a momentary pang of guilt at making her uncomfortable. She was Sophia's friend and none of my past had anything to do with her. "I'm sorry," I said, taking her hand. "It's a pleasure to meet you." I glanced over her shoulder at Cane. "You must be one hell of a special woman for Cane to call you his fiancé. When's the wedding?"

"We've decided to wait until after the baby is born." I nodded. Thea bit her bottom lip, and stepped back to Cane, grabbing onto his arm and pulling him forward. "Sophia," she said. "Cane. You've spoken on the phone, of course, but I guess that's different from meeting in person."

Cane nodded his head at Sophia and gave her a wry smile before rubbing the back of his neck. "I, umm, hadn't meant for our first meeting to be so dramatic," he said. "It's great to finally meet you."

Sophia looked torn between protecting me and driving away her new friend. Before she had the chance to decide, I interjected. "Cane is Caleb's brother."

Sophia's eyes widened in shock.

"You don't have to worry. I won't mention a thing to Caleb. And despite what you might have heard, he would never hurt Amber," he said to Sophia before giving me a pointed look. "It's actually the other way around."

"You have no idea what you're talking about," Sophia said as anger clouded her face.

I wanted to scream at her to calm down, to stop before she spilled my secrets. I was about to say something when Charlie chose that not-so-perfect time to run into the room.

"Mommy," she said, waving a teddy in the air. "Lookit."

My heart leaped into my throat as I bent to scoop her into my arms. After she'd waved the teddy in my face for a second, she decided to introduce it to the rest of the room.

"It's so cute," Thea said as her eyes darted from me to the bear. "Does it have a name?"

At that moment, I knew she must know a little about my history in the same way I knew a little about hers. She'd just never put Sophia's Amber and Caleb's Amber together as the same person before. Sophia must have realized the same thing too, as she gave Thea an almost imperceptible shake of her head. Thea, in turn, gave me a reassuring smile, and I realized that no matter how much she knew, she wouldn't share it.

"Teddy," Charlie said. "My bear from Aunt Caroline."

"It's a really lovely bear," Thea said, smiling.

Charlie turned to Cane as if seeing him for the first time. "Big bear," she said, before reaching out to his neck. Her hand stopped and she turned it, lifting her head high before stroking her own neck. "Paint body. Mommy, me paint."

"Oh, no, no, no," I said, pulling her hand down. "You are

doing no such thing."

Cane chuckled. "You are way too small to paint your body," he said. "It's a grown-up thing."

"Aunt Sophia say Charlie big girl. Big girl can paint."

Cane laughed. "It looks like you'll have your hands full there when she grows up," he said before turning to look me in the eye. As soon as he did, they darted back to Charlie and then to me again. I could practically hear the thought-clogs circling in his mind. "Jesus, Amber. Charlie?" he said and shook his head. "How could you be so cruel to keep this from Caleb?" He turned to Thea and then Franc and nodded. "If you'll excuse me. I should have left when you said to go." With that, he turned and stormed out the front door.

Charlie buried her head in my neck, and I pulled her close, tears falling from my eyes. "Cane, please?" I called after him, my voice breaking on the words.

Thea rubbed Charlie on the back. "Don't worry," she said. "Leave him to me. Everything will be fine."

"Don't tell," I said.

"I won't. Trust me." Thea left the house hot on Cane's trail.

I stared after them, not sure what to do. "I'm so sorry, Sophia. I always cause you so much trouble. This was meant to be a celebration for your wedding."

She rubbed my back in much the same way as Thea had

rubbed Charlie's. "It's no trouble at all."

After a few minutes, Thea returned, knocking on the open door before stepping tentatively inside. "Cane won't say anything," she said. "At least not straight away. But it will eat him up inside to keep this from Caleb."

"I know."

Caroline stepped forwards and reached for Charlie. "You know what I completely forgot about?" she said. "In the backyard, we have the best apple tree in the whole of Castle Rock. How would you like to help me pick some apples, and then we can bake a pie?"

Charlie nodded and allowed Caroline to take her away again.

Thea sat on the sofa next to me, while Franc cleared his throat and excused himself. He went to the kitchen and returned a second later, carrying a couple of beers he must have grabbed from the fridge, and took them outside to join Cane.

"How did you get him to agree?" I asked Thea.

She glanced from me to Sophia and smiled. "Cane's a big softy at heart. He doesn't want to see anyone hurt."

I shook my head and gave a wry laugh. "I'm not sure anyone within a two-hundred-mile radius has ever called Cane a softy before."

"Sure, they have. Cherrie does it all the time."

"Cherrie." I sighed. "There's another name I haven't heard in a long time."

"You still okay?" Sophia asked. "I never meant for this to happen. I just didn't realize Thea would be connected to Forever Midnight in any way."

I patted her on the knee. "It's okay. I suppose when I agreed to come, a part of me wondered if I'd cross their paths. It's a small town, after all. I just hadn't expected Cane to walk straight in the front door five minutes after I arrived."

Thea looked to her feet. "I know it's not my place to say anything," she said after a moment. "But maybe this is for the best—" she glanced at Sophia "—The timing sucks. But... well, I know a little bit about what happened."

My eyes darted to Sophia. "It's fine. You're friends. Friends share things with each other. I know a bit about your past too," I added, addressing Thea.

"The world can be a shitty place." She rubbed her baby bump. "But it can be amazing too, and I have Cane now. I've dealt with my past and moved on. Maybe... maybe it's time for you to do the same thing."

"Thea's right," Sophia said, but she'd always thought I should have come clean with Caleb.

"It could start a war," I said.

"Maybe." Thea sighed. "And I'm not going to pretend to be happy about that. But some wars are just."

I looked at her earnest face and saw what drew both Cane and Sophia to her. She'd been tortured and beaten for almost a decade by her psychopathic stepbrother, and none of her compassion for other people had faded.

But I didn't have her strength.

I stood and paced the room. "I can't," I said after a moment. "How can I face him after all this time? He must hate me."

Thea shook her head. "I didn't know the Caleb you knew, but I know the man he is now, and I can tell you for sure, he doesn't hate you."

"How? How can you know that?"

She looked me in the eyes. "He's too angry at you. Too hurt and broken, not to love you."

"Don't be fooled." I scoffed. "Caleb's good at angry."

"He is. They both are." Her gaze shifted to the front door where Franc stood next to Cane. The pair of them knocked back their beer and chatted, for all the world, like old buddies. A smile twitched at the corner of Thea's mouth before she said, "In all the time you've been gone, Caleb has never looked at another woman. Not even for a throw-away, one-night stand."

"I doubt that." The Caleb I knew had one hell of a healthy appetite for sex. That didn't disappear overnight.

"You might doubt it, but it's the truth. At least, that's what Cane believes." Thea stood and placed her hand on my arm. "You named your baby Charlie," she said. "His dad's name. That has to mean something."

Sophia stood and gave me a look. That was the one thing I'd kept from her, knowing that I'd get another lecture about returning home and facing up to everything that happened if she found out.

"But I don't know if she's his." My hand flew to my mouth and I tried to stop the tears from falling again.

Sophia was there in a second, pulling me in for a hug. "I know, chica, I know."

"He won't care," Thea said.

She meant it nicely, but that's what I feared the most now, that Caleb wouldn't not only care that Charlie wasn't his, but he also wouldn't care if she was.

I huffed out a breath and pulled away from Sophia. "You think Cane could do me one more favor?" I asked. Thea nodded. "Ask him to tell Caleb I'm here and want to speak with him but ask him not to mention Charlie. I need to tell him about her myself." If he showed. Though why would he if I'd caused him as much pain as both Thea and Cane seemed to think I had?

CHAPTER TWO

Caleb

I pulled my bike up along the road from the bungalow and stared at the building unsure what to do. When Cane arrived at the clubhouse and told me he'd seen Amber, my first reaction was one of disbelief, my second was to punch him in the fucking face for bringing her name up. Thank fuck, I didn't. My third was a desperate need to see her.

She wanted to see me too. At least, that's what Cane said. If he was any other fucker, I'd doubt his word, but Cane knew what Amber's leaving did to me. He saw how she ripped out my heart and stomped on it with her perfect size eights, digging her heels in as she left.

And now what? She was fucking back and wanted to talk. I sucked in a deep breath before letting it out again, my nostrils flaring.

Torn up inside, I'd searched for Amber for days after she left me. I went to her work, only to find she'd left her job. Visited every one of her friends I knew, but she'd dumped them as surely as she dumped me. She even ditched her phone number and sold her car at a loss to make a quick deal and get out of town. If she had any family, I would never have given up, but Amber was an only child whose parents died when she was away at college. She had no other family to speak of. Other than me.

It used to rile me when she said family came first with me. Of course, they fucking did. And Amber, Cane, and Dad were the closest family I had. I would have done anything for each and every one of them. I should have known then that she never felt the same way about me. She never would have whined about it otherwise.

What was the maneuver in that Tarantino series? The one the Bride used to kill Bill with? The Five Point Palm Exploding Heart Technique. That's it; that's what it felt like. I'd just lost Dad and then the shit with Amber. She couldn't have done a better fucking job of kicking me out of her life if she'd killed me, and there were times it felt like she had. Like my heart had fucking exploded.

Hell, there were times when I wished I was dead. But my brothers kept me going.

I clenched my fists, pushed them deep into my forehead, and

tried to still the bubbling rage that wanted to break free and stop me being hurt again.

Our last telephone conversation played over and over in my head. She was worried about me, or at least, I'd thought she was at the time. She'd wanted to go away. I'd refused. I should have given her what she wanted. I would have done anything to keep her in my life.

It was a difficult time, and with dad being slain, I thought I had to stay with Cane. He was my baby brother. He needed me. We needed to catch the fucker who took out dad. Only after we saw him in his grave would we be able to properly grieve. I could have understood if Amber had told me that was the problem, if she'd said she couldn't deal with what Cane and I had to do. But no, she chose the option of fucking ghosting me instead. She avoided my calls, and when I got home from Mexico, all her things were gone.

She left me a fucking note. *'Sorry. Don't try to find me.'* Six simple fucking words that damn near destroyed my life. Yet, despite them, I had tried. Tried and failed. It took me a few sleepless days, but I finally got her message loud and clear. Though, maybe, if I hadn't given up, I wouldn't be sitting on my bike like a frightened pussy, too fucking scared to knock on a door.

Some fucking tough guy, I was.

I shook my head and focused on the house. I'd spent years reliving the times I'd had with Amber, trying to figure out what the fuck went wrong.

Lord knows I was — am — a fucking prick. I've never been easy to live with, but...

I hissed out a breath and clutched my hands to my head.

Fuck this!

I couldn't see her. I couldn't look at her perfect face or see her curious eyes, always burning with questions, and not fucking die inside all over again.

I was about to start my engine when a patrol car pulled up alongside my bike and Officer Tom Davenport, patted the side of his door through the window.

"Everything okay?" He asked.

"Everything's fine, Tom. How are things with you?"

"Same old, same old." He glanced up and down the street. "Any particular reason you're scoping this place out?"

I scoffed and shook my head. "You know better than that," I said. "Not my style. I'm visiting an old friend, that's all."

"Yeah? Anyone I know?"

"Not that I know of. Her name's Amber Gerald. She's in the bungalow if you want to check out my story." I nodded to the house.

Tom's gaze followed my own and he stared at it for a while

as if assessing his next move. A part of me wanted him to fucking knock on the door and draw Amber out. At least then the decision would be made for me. Instead, he tapped the side of his cruiser again and told me to take care before moving on.

I debated pulling away and following him but stopped myself and took a deep breath. If I didn't speak to Amber now, I'd be adding another regret to my long list.

I kicked my bike on its stand and stood tall. My muscles twitched and I tried to force myself to relax.

A car honked as I stepped into the road. I scowled at the driver, ready to punch him out if he honked again. He put his foot down and sped away with a nervous backward glance. I turned back to the bungalow in time to see Amber stepping out of the front door.

All the air swept from my lungs and my chest clenched painfully at the sight of her. Despite the passing years, she hadn't aged a day. Her simple jeans and T-shirt hugged her figure like a second skin. Blonde hair cascaded over her shoulder in a wave of curls, highlighted like a halo in the afternoon sun. She pushed it behind her ear. Her shoulders lifted and sagged as though she'd taken a deep breath. She sucked in her lips. My dick jumped to fucking attention.

I wanted to run over to her, scoop her into my arms, and never let her go. I craved her voice, the dimples that appeared in her cheeks when she smiled, the warmth of her body next to mine. But fear that her apparition would disappear and I'd never see her again stopped my steps.

Amber came to me, her eyes drifting from the floor to my face and back again. She stopped a foot away. I could reach out and touch her, but didn't. Neither of us said a word for countless seconds. I just stared at her like some fucking psychopath in a horror movie while she looked at the ground.

She clutched her arms across her chest. "I'm so sorry." Her voice trembled and she lifted her head, her eyes meeting mine for the first time.

Any anger, any grudge, I might have held, fled from me. Her gaze wasn't the carefree one I knew. It held the same look I saw in Thea's eyes the first time I met her. She was trying to escape Cane and return to her stepbrother to save Cherrie. A look that said life had kicked you in the gut and the pain was too much to live with.

"Jesus, Amber," I said. "What the fuck happened?" I stepped forward and pulled her into my arms. She let me. Her head fell against my chest and great sobbing gasps came from her throat.

I stroked her hair and closed my eyes, breathing her in. I knew now why she had returned. Someone had hurt her, and she needed me. A pang of resentment struck deep inside, but I shoved it down. It didn't matter that Amber had only returned because she knew I would protect her. All that mattered was making sure she was safe and keeping her that way.

"Tell me which fucker needs killing and I'll see it done," I said.

Amber's shaking stilled and she pulled away from me, wiping beneath her eyes with the backs of her fingers. She huffed out a breath and glanced over her shoulder at the house before turning back to face me. "We should talk," she said. "But somewhere else."

"Where do you want to go?"

"I don't know. Anywhere." She shrugged before turning her gaze to the butte in the distance. "How about the trailhead up by Castle Rock?"

I nodded and climbed on my bike, doing my best not to react. That was the last place I took her before Dad died. We'd parked the bike up, hiked the trail, and climbed on top of the rock. We spent the entire night talking with the lights of the town twinkling around us.

"Hop on," I said and patted the seat. Amber slipped behind me and circled her arms around my waist.

My heart thundered, but I kept my cool and steered my bike toward the Rock Park parking lot.

Despite the lateness of the afternoon, the sun still sat high in the sky, and several cars were parked in the lot. Castle Rock was a heavily used trail. A young couple sat at a picnic table beneath the large shelter. The guy pulled his girl away as soon as he saw us arrive on the bike.

I huffed out a breath. It was strangely comforting to know I could still scare some fucker just by being present.

I parked up the bike and waited for Amber to get off before joining her. Neither of us was dressed for hiking, but it was an easy trail, and it wasn't as if we'd climb the rock. Not during fucking daylight hours anyway.

Amber was tense and I knew she was regretting her decision to come here with me. Ignoring her discomfort, I pointed toward the trail between the trees.

"Let's walk," I said. "If nothing else, it will help clear our heads." Amber agreed and, without a backward glance to see if I was following, headed along the trail.

We passed a young family. The woman grabbed her child's hand to keep her near. The man, a slim guy wearing beige shorts, a T-shirt and a fanny-pack, turned his attention to Amber with a concerned look on his face. She smiled at him, and he glanced at me. We never looked as though we belonged together. Amber was far too much of a fucking princess for the likes of me.

I liked him. He was a man who'd step in if he thought Amber was in trouble. Even if I was five times his fucking size and likely to lay him out flat with a single punch.

I turned around and showed him the patch on my back. "Caleb Landon, Forever Midnight MC, and this is Amber Gerald. We're old friends," I said to reassure him. "You have my word, she's in no danger."

Amber reached toward me and clasped on to my hand. "We're fine," she said, and he tipped his head to her. "Ma'am, Sir. Have a good walk."

"Thanks, brother." As we continued on the trail and out of view of the family, I half expected Amber to pull her hand from mine, but she didn't.

The trail hadn't changed much in the four years since I'd last been up it. The incline was a little steeper than I remembered, and it had been dark then, so the wildflowers hadn't been visible the way they were now. Although, the sweet scent remained the same. It was the heat that was different. No cool night air refreshed my face. Instead, the sun baked me inside my jacket like a potato in foil. Despite not wanting to break my contact with Amber, I pulled my hand from hers to remove my jacket. My T-shirt followed suit. As soon as I'd lifted it over my head, I noted Amber staring at me.

"You're bigger than I remember," she said.

"You're just the same," I answered.

She stepped forward and ran her hand along my arm. Her touch lingered. "That's new," she said, noting the rose and thorns.

"I got it after you left."

She pulled her hand away and clutched it to herself. A group of five hikers rounded the bend in front of us. Amber closed her eyes and swallowed before opening them again. "This isn't the best place to talk," she said.

Before she had the chance to say anything else, bird shit fell from the sky and landed on her head and shoulder with a momentous splatter. She froze with a horrified look on her face. "Just fucking perfect," she said and burst out laughing.

For the first time, I saw a trace of the Amber I knew, and laughed too. "Yo, brothers," I said, calling to the group of hikers. "Any of you spare some water?"

"Sure, got a bottle here." The lead walker reached behind his back and pulled a bottle out of his rucksack. Amber clutched her mouth, trying to still her laughter.

"Thanks," I said, taking it from him.

"Yes, thank you," Amber added as embarrassment colored her cheeks.

I unscrewed the cap and asked Amber to tilt her head. She did and I poured water from the bottle over her head, doing my best to rinse the shit from her hair, while wiping it off her shoulder with my T-shirt.

"That's the best I can do. You're gonna need to wash it out

properly." I cleared my throat. "You can shower at my place," I dared saying. "Then we can grab a stiff drink and have that talk."

Amber was quiet for so long, I wondered if she'd heard what I said, but I realized she was debating if it was wise to come home with me or not.

Fuck! I was wondering exactly the same thing. But Amber was right, this was a bad place to talk. And I needed to talk. I needed to know why she'd left me the way she did, and who had hurt her and brought her back into my life now. We needed somewhere we wouldn't be interrupted, and no place was better than home for that.

CHAPTER THREE

Amber

Caleb wasn't the man I remembered. Something inside had changed, he seemed harder, yet more timid at the same time. Cane was right, I had hurt him. When I'd left, I knew I would, but not this much. I thought he'd move on and find someone new within a matter of months, if not weeks. At least that's what I'd told myself to lessen the guilt of my actions.

I'd heard him arrive and stop his bike outside the house. I waited an eternity for him to come to the door, but no knock sounded. My stomach twisted in knots and my heart clenched. After forty minutes had passed and I'd twitched the curtains to look at him for the hundredth time, Charlie asked who I was looking at.

"An old friend," I said.

"Why don't you say hello?" she asked, and I realized that's

exactly what I had to do.

He'd dared to come, even if he hadn't made it past the end of the street, and if I didn't speak to him now, there was the possibility Cane would do it in my stead, and he didn't know half the story.

"That's a good idea, but I might have to go away with him for a while. Will you be okay with Aunt Sophia?"

Sophia pulled Charlie up onto her lap. Her parents had left to visit friends for a couple of hours and only the three of us remained. "We are going to eat bad food and watch a movie in bed. You take all the time you need." With that, she bopped Charlie on the nose.

Charlie giggled, and I gave her a big hug before leaving. I knew she'd be fine in Sophia's care. She and her parents had been my lifeline over the years and had come to the city to take care of Charlie on a regular basis.

Taking a deep breath, I opened the door, but nearly stalled when I heard the honking of a horn. Those steps toward him were the second hardest of my life. The hardest were the ones I took walking away.

Then, I'd feared he'd come home and take one look at me and know what had happened. He was already hurting and would start a war with the Feral Sons, for me. I couldn't have that. But more than that, I couldn't have him look at me and see how much it hurt. I thought time had healed that pain, but the second he looked into my eyes, he asked me what the fuck had happened. He saw exactly what I feared he would.

He should have been angry, should have screamed at me for leaving the way I did, but all I saw was concern. Maybe Thea was right, maybe there was love there too. Everything came crashing down. I wanted him to hold me. I wanted to blurt out everything, but I was too afraid of what would happen if I did.

The last thing I thought would happen was that a bird would poop on my head and I'd end up at our old house.

Caleb started tidying away a few empty beer bottles and cans as soon as we entered. The house seemed colder than it used to. The furnishings were drab, and the color had left the place. Questions burned behind Caleb's eyes, but I couldn't stomach answering them. Not yet.

"Let me shower and get cleaned up," I said before darting up the stairs and into the wet room.

I looked in the mirror and realized what a complete mess I was. Caleb had done a good job of rinsing the poop from my hair, but it was clumped together and slimy where it hit, and the smudge mark on my top didn't look any better. Here I was, looking a state, and Caleb was the hottest I'd ever seen him. It wasn't my memory playing tricks on me when I said he looked bigger. He'd definitely gained some bulk. And when he took his shirt off... I thought I'd faint into his arms at the sight of his abs, and don't get me started on those pecs.

I stripped from my dirty clothes and turned on the shower, running it for a few minutes before stepping beneath. Closing my eyes, I allowed the hot stream of water to wash away all the years, all the bad memories that plagued my mind. Instead, I shampooed my hair and focused on the good times we'd had in this house, this shower.

An image of Caleb naked and wet flashed through my mind. I tried to latch on to the memory, to hear him laugh and say my name in that deep, sexy voice of his. I tried to remember what it felt like to have him inside me. As I'd done countless times over the years when thinking of Caleb, I reached down and massaged my clit. I circled my nub, stroking harder and faster. Pleasure swirled through my core and a soft moan broke from my lips. I placed my hand against the wall to steady my balance. Water sluiced down my back and I pictured it sluicing down Caleb's and over the curve of his bottom.

Feeling at home, even though I hadn't called this house my home in years, I abandoned my clit and pushed my fingers inside me. Pleasure swirled through my core, and I wished they were Caleb's fingers pounding into me, instead of my own.

My core clenched and the promised jolts of pleasure were moments away. Extending the moment, I returned to my clit and worked it with my fingers at a frantic pace.

Caleb's presence manifested as the door opened behind me, but before I had the chance to react, his hand reached down and stilled my fingers. "Let me," he said.

I froze and turned to see him fully clothed. "We shouldn't."

"Do you want me to leave?"

My rational mind told me I should say yes and that this shouldn't happen as it would only complicate things more. But what had I expected when I came home with him? What had I wanted when I'd started touching myself in the shower?

Caleb cocked his head and looked at my lips. I stared into deep brown eyes so like Charlie's they made my heart burst. The need in them mirrored my own.

"Why don't you hate me?" I asked.

Caleb gave a wry smile and shook the water from his face. "I could never hate you."

His lips met mine in a rush, and he devoured me, plunging his tongue inside. He tasted of cola and cherries. The room spun on its axis and I worried I might slip and fall, but Caleb pushed me against the wall and looked at me. His clothes plastered to his body in the stream of water. His gaze never left my eyes, but his hands cupped my breasts. His fingers pulled and tweaked at my tightened nipples. He dipped his head and sucked one into his mouth. I hissed out a breath as his needy tongue circled the bud, sending a shiver down my spine and making my core flex in anticipation.

In all the years I'd been away, I'd dreamed of a reconciliation, hoped there was a chance for us. But over time, that hope faded. I'd ended what we had, thrown it away like yesterday's newspaper. I'd shut Caleb out and built a wall around my heart to keep it safe. But as Caleb's fingers found my throbbing clit, that wall came crashing down.

After all this time, I needed more. I fumbled with his T-shirt, trying to get it over his head even though the water had glued it to his body. Caleb helped, and my fingers found the buttons on his jeans. Within moments, they were in a sopping heap on the wet room floor.

I pulled back and looked at his cock. Just like the rest of him, it was bigger than I remembered. Its slit glistened and water dripped from the tip. I licked my lips.

"Ask and it's yours," Caleb said.

Heat flooded my body, and I play-slapped him on the chest. "What?"

"I want to make you fucking beg."

My core pulsed with need. I was ready to beg now, but cocky Caleb was in full flow and I loved it when he teased me. "It's not gonna happen," I said as a smile played at the edge of my mouth.

We both knew it would.

Without another word, Caleb grabbed me by the hips and hoisted me in the air. I squealed as he spun me around the wet room and my bare ass landed on the cold sheen of the countertop next to the washbasin. He spread my legs and I waited wide-eyed as he kneeled on the floor between them.

The soft touch of his skin, and the faint trace of bristle, tickled my inner thighs sending shivers up my spine. He pushed my legs further apart as wide as they could go.

God, I'd missed this. Missed him.

"You're gonna beg," he muttered, and I giggled wondering just how long I could hold out before he proved right.

He pressed his hot lips to my folds, and his tongue reached out for more. He teased, flicking along the length of my eager opening, grazing my clit and shooting electricity through it. A spasm rocked my body, driving me out of my mind.

I clasped his head in my hands, and pulled him closer, wanting more. Caleb withdrew his lips and slipped two fingers into my wet core. My muscles clamped around them, willing them in further. He pumped into me, twisting and scissoring his fingers, making me writhe and jerk my hips from the countertop to meet him. He pinned me down and fucked me with his fingers for a while longer before withdrawing and licking my wetness from them.

The pulse between my legs pounded, begging for him to do

more. I growled in frustration. Caleb only smiled in return.

"You ready to beg, yet?" he asked.

I chuckled. "I think it's you who's going to do the begging." I pulled him up and took his position on the floor, then wrapped my hand around his thick erection and squeezed. It pulsed in my hand, making me want it inside me even more.

I licked along his slit. Caleb hissed through his teeth. I smiled and did it again, flicking my tongue back down and making him shudder.

My nipples tightened, feeling harder than ever, as I ran my tongue along the deliciously long length of his dick before slipping it inside my mouth and sucking on the thick head. I couldn't stop the moan of my own at the taste of his precum. My hand slid to his balls. I massaged them between my fingers as my mouth bobbed up and down his length and my tongue explored the ridges around his cock head. He rocked to meet me, but I pushed him back. A smile curved my lips as I pulled away with one final brush of my tongue against his slit.

Caleb growled and my smile deepened.

"Are you ready to beg, yet?" I asked.

Caleb groaned, but returned my smile and hoisted me back onto the countertop. He flung my legs apart and licked and sucked with animalistic fervor at my free-flowing juices. I bucked my hips, and, this time, he let me.

He pulled back and looked at me, his brown eyes twinkling.

God! I could get lost in those depths... again.

I had to remind myself that this was a fleeting moment, things would change as soon as we'd talked. After that, he'd never look at me the same way again.

Caleb stood, and for a moment, he did nothing but take in the sight of me as though etching me into his brain. My cheeks flushed. My body... my heart would always beg for Caleb. But some things are just not meant to be. He knew it as much as I did.

Caleb closed the small space between us, gripped his cock, and guided himself to my waiting core. My breath hitched, ready for him to pummel into me, but instead, he teased my entry with its tip. I closed my eyes and remembered the feeling of him buried deep inside. When he pulled forward to tease again, I bucked to meet him, but he pinned me down again and delved two fingers inside instead. He alternated between pumping his fingers inside me and teasing me with the head of his cock, never pushing it more than an inch inside. I bit back a scream of frustration. No longer able to bear his denial of what I wanted... what I needed, I relented.

"Please," I begged.

Caleb leaned forward and kissed me. I tasted myself on his lips. He pulled back and sucked in one of my nipples. His hand pinched and rolled the other between his fingers. My back arched and sparks of pleasure shot to my clit.

"You call that begging," Caleb muttered between a suck and a nip.

"Please." Ragged breaths heaved from my lungs. "I want you inside me. All of you." I raised an eyebrow. "Would you prefer me on my hands and knees... begging?" I asked and licked my lips.

Caleb smiled, and my legs trembled as he positioned himself at my aching entry. With agonizing slowness, he pushed the length of his throbbing cock inside, stretching me wide with his massive girth. Just when I thought I couldn't take anymore, he thrust deeper. I screamed in pleasure and clasped onto his bulging arms.

He drew back until just the tip of him was inside me again.

"Please," I said. "Fuck me."

Our eyes locked. Caleb gave me a devilish grin that made my heart melt. He drove in, again and again, reaching the deepest parts of me. I pulled him close, clasping my hands around his neck and burying my head next to his for fear of losing myself. Tingling ripples of pleasure, just on the brink of becoming pain, shot through my entire being. "More," I moaned. "Harder."

Caleb obliged, pumping into me harder and faster. "I can't hold back," he said. "I fucking can't..."

Every muscle in his body tensed, and my core clenched, milking his climax as I shuddered and wave after wave of pleasure imploded within me. Caleb drove into me, one final time, pinning me to the wall so hard I thought we might fall through. Our breaths were fast and desperate. Caleb withdrew, but sealed my lips with another kiss before pulling away, hovering mere centimeters from my face.

"Well, that was an interesting development," he said before kissing me again, long and hard.

I kissed him back, not wanting the moment to end or for reality to set in. But my senses kicked in and I knew I had to stop things before I broke both our hearts, again.

I pushed away, stood, and turned off the shower. Steam filled the room in a misty haze, yet despite its warmth, I shivered.

Caleb noticed and handed me the towel from the rack.

"We should probably have that talk now," I said.

CHAPTER FOUR

Caleb

*F*uck! What had I done? I knew it was a mistake to bring Amber here, how dangerous it would be to have her in our… my home, but I hadn't cared, and when I'd walked up the stairs to find her a clean shirt and heard her moan in the wet room, I knew what she was doing and couldn't resist opening the door. But the look she gave me as soon as we were through spoke volumes. The quick fuck had been her way of thanking me for whatever the hell it was she needed me to do. She was going to break my heart all fucking over again, and I opened the door and invited her in.

The stupid thing was, I was gonna do whatever the hell she needed me to. What choice did I have? I'd never forgive myself if I wasn't there to help her. Damn it! She may not love me, but I would always love her.

I slammed two bottles of beer down on the counter and kicked the fridge door shut. Amber was ready to talk. She'd tell me why she was here, I'd fix her problem, and then fucking what? She'd be gone again. I huffed out a breath and tried to relax the tension building in my shoulders.

Footsteps sounded upstairs and I knew Amber had to be on her way down. I rolled my shoulder, and buttoned up my jeans, wishing for all the world, I'd grabbed myself a T-shirt before coming downstairs.

The kitchen door inched open and Amber entered. Her wet hair hung loose over one shoulder, and the top I'd given to her had damp patches that clung to her breasts. I closed my mouth and gave my head a mental shake. It was time to talk. Nothing more. Nothing less. I should have stuck to that premise when she'd first arrived.

I grabbed one of the beers and popped the top before handing it to Amber.

"Thanks," she said, and as she took a swig, I saw that her hands were shaking.

I searched her perfect face. Worry etched her features, but she refused to look me in the eyes.

I opened my bottle and almost downed it in one gulp before going to grab another. Amber placed hers on the counter.

"It's hot in here," she said. "You think we can take a walk out back?"

"I thought you wanted to talk," I said and closed the fridge forgoing the second beer.

"I-I do. I just think it will be easier if I do it while we're walking."

I nodded and excused myself to grab a T-shirt and my boots. We headed out the back door as soon as I returned. The large garden backed onto part of the State Park; we made our way through the bushes and headed to a path we'd walked a thousand times before. Night-time bleached the landscape of color and the tree-branches loomed overhead as though sleepy and stretching toward each other. The only sound was the shuffling of our feet on the dirt trail and the cry of the Great Horned Owl as it soared through the sky.

To my surprise, Amber reached out, grabbed my hand and squeezed. I squeezed back.

"Whatever you need me to do, I'll do it," I said in an attempt to reassure her. "No questions asked."

We continued in silence for a short time until Amber seemed to come to a decision and took a deep breath. "I just need you to do one thing," she said, her voice breaking.

I pulled her to a stop and held her face in both my hands. Dampness stained her cheeks and I realized that she'd been crying silent tears. I wiped them away and stared into her eyes. "I said, whatever you need, and I meant it."

She gave me a small smile and nodded her head before reaching for my hand again and continuing to walk. "You have to promise not to act on what I tell you, at least, not right away. Process what I say and then act with a rational mind. Don't go off half-cocked."

A sour tang hit the back of my mouth as I realized she was scared of how I'd react. "I promise," I said.

Still, we walked. Despite the monotony of our pace and the monochrome of our surroundings, my heart thundered and my mind whirled. Tension practically jumped along Amber's skin. I turned to face her and by the moonlight, saw another tear roll down her cheek. She wiped it away with the back of her free hand.

"Do you remember our last telephone conversation?" she asked, her voice clogged with emotion.

"I'll never forget it," I answered.

"Something happened that night. On the way home." A rolling dread churned my stomach and made my chest feel as though someone held it in a vice, but I held my tongue and waited for Amber to continue. "A group of bikers rammed me off the road. My tire burst. My phone was dead."

Her voice trailed off and her gaze turned to our

surroundings for a second before she leaned over and placed her hands on her knees, swallowing hard and shaking as emotions overwhelmed her. I knelt beside her and rubbed her back. She fell to the ground.

"I couldn't do anything," she said. "I couldn't stop him." She crumbled in my arms and I sat on the ground, my heart screaming, and held her tight.

I stroked her hair and tried to remain calm for Amber's sake, but my jaw rooted, and I became almost breathless with anger.

"What happened, baby?" I asked, and knowing now that it had to be connected, "Why did you leave?"

Amber pulled back and stared at her empty hands as they trembled. The dull light cast her face in shadows, but her pain was evident to my eyes. "He pulled me from the car and raped me."

Anger ripped through my insides like a fucking tornado. Someone had raped my angel. I wanted to stand and pace, punch something, someone. Instead, I swallowed that anger like it was a stick of dynamite, and promised myself, when the time was right, I'd direct it at the right person and let it explode. I wished I could make everything better, but this wasn't about someone I could protect her from, this was about someone who had already hurt her, and I couldn't do anything about that but kill the fucker.

"Why didn't you tell me?" I blurted, but as I said the words dread shook me to the core. She'd said that bikers rammed her off the road. "Was it someone in Forever Midnight? Was that why you left?" I couldn't process the thought that someone I considered a brother could hurt Amber, but it explained everything.

"No," she said after clearing her throat. "It was someone from the Feral Son's. There were six of them there, but only one… only one… hurt me."

I pulled her close and held her. "Do you know his name?" I asked. She shook her head. My mind whirled and a certainty stabbed me through the heart. "He hurt you because of me, didn't he?"

She nodded and I died inside all over again. No wonder she left. How could she stand to fucking look at me after what happened?

"I'm so sorry," I said, although the words were inadequate. Even if Amber didn't know who had attacked her, at that moment, I fucking did.

Amber took a deep breath and pulled away again. "He had a tattoo on his neck," she said, confirming my suspicions. "A lion with a crown. He told me to get a good look and tell you exactly who hurt me."

"Leo," I said and instantly fucking regretted it when Amber

crumpled again. She fell against me and cried until she was completely wrung out.

CHAPTER FIVE

Amber

F lashing red lights greeted us as soon as we turned the corner, casting the street in a macabre and dangerous light. A patrol car was parked in front of the bungalow.

For the entire trip back to Sophia's, I'd clung onto Caleb's back and tried to focus on anything but the name of my attacker. Leo. I should have known with his stupid tattoo, but that was the least of my worries now. I jumped from the bike, not waiting for Caleb to bring it to a complete stop and raced towards the house. All I could think was that something had happened to Charlie.

Sophia emerged, wearing fluffy slippers in the form of bunny rabbits and a dressing-. From all appearances, she probably had very little on underneath. An officer followed behind her, and before I had the chance to say anything, she ran toward me and pulled me in for a hug.

"She's fine. We're all fine. She's still asleep in the bedroom. I swear that kid would sleep through a rock concert."

Although relief surged through me at her words, I itched to run inside and wake Charlie to see for myself that she was fine, but knew I'd only scare her if I did. Instead, I let out a breath I hadn't realized I'd been holding, pulled away from Sophia, and glanced over my shoulder at Caleb. The officer had walked over to him and they were talking in the street. From the looks of things, they already knew each other.

"I told Caleb about the attack, but still haven't mentioned Charlie," I said. My way of asking Sophia not to bring her up in Caleb's presence. Not yet. "What the hell happened?"

"We had some visitors. A group of assholes on motorbikes thought it would be funny to holler at the house while revving their engines and generally making a commotion in the street." She glanced at the officer and huffed out a breath. "They threw a brick through the window." She looked like she wanted to say something more but bit her lip as if she was keeping the words locked inside.

I was about to ask what she wasn't telling me when my gaze roamed over the house, and for the first time, I noticed the shattered window and broken glass and nearly broke down all over again. I didn't need my gut instinct to tell me this was all my fault; it was as plane as the nose on my face.

"Hey," Sophia said, pulling me in for another hug. "No crying, chica. We're fine. Everything's fine. We didn't even call the cops. You can thank one of the neighbors for that."

"You should have called the cops," I said as I pulled back and looked at her face. "It was the Feral Son's, wasn't it? You know what they can do. The second they entered the street, you should have called the cops and hidden. Promise me. If they come again, you'll make sure you and your family are safe."

"Ladies," the officer said as he and Caleb walked towards us. "Ms. Cortez. I just wanted to double-check the insignia details on the bikers you saw. Are you sure it was an animal skull and not a human one?" He twirled his finger in the air and motioned for Caleb to turn around. Caleb obliged, displaying the Forever Midnight MC patch on his jacket.

"Positive," Sophia said. "I can tell the difference between an animal skull and a human one. Besides the fact the other had large canine teeth on full display, it also didn't have wings or a full-moon backing it up."

The officer let out a deep sigh and tapped his pen against the pad in his hand before pointing it at Caleb. "You and I both know that even though Forever Midnight didn't do anything here tonight, your presence speaks volumes to the fact that they are somehow involved." With that, he took a deep breath and put his pen and pad away. "I'll send a patrol car around to check up on you folks every couple of hours. If these guys return, I want you to call in straight away."

"No need, Tom," Caleb said, confirming my guess that he was already acquainted with the officer. "They won't be staying here."

Sophia glanced at me. "I'll call Ben. My fiancé," she added at the blank look on Caleb's face. "We can stay with him in Twin Cedars."

"Not a fucking chance," Caleb growled. "I need you somewhere the brothers can protect you."

Sophia looked as though she was about to say something, but I put up my hand to stop her. "We can talk it through and figure out the details," I said.

"Well," Tom gave Caleb another pointed look, "keep me in the loop and let me know what you decide. The offer to have a patrol car come around is still on the table." He crooked his finger at Caleb and motioned him to step aside. "A word."

Sophia watched them as they moved away but I couldn't keep my gaze from her face. This was meant to be the happiest time of her life. In a few days, she was set to marry, after that she was jetting off to the Bahamas for her honeymoon. Sophia and her parents had done so much to help me over the years, and I couldn't be more grateful, but for now, I had to distance myself from them to keep them safe. I only wished I could send

Charlie away with them, but that would be too much to ask, and I couldn't bear to be without her. No. It was time to tell Caleb everything.

I followed Sophia's gaze and turned my attention to Caleb and the officer, Tom. They were still talking, but every so often Caleb would glance my way. He gave me an almost imperceptible nod and a smile. He'd been holding things together since I'd told him about my attack, but now just as I had then, I could feel the anger and frustration coming off him in waves. He was ready to kill Leo, and God help me, I was ready to let him.

"He's more intense than I imagined," Sophia said, drawing my attention back to her. "Like a tight coil ready to spring." A sly smile played at the edge of her lips. "Bigger too. You never did tell me just how big, chica," she said and gave me a playful nudge with her elbow.

Despite everything, I laughed. Sophia always had a way of bringing a smile out of me even in the direst of circumstances. I wish I had her positive outlook on life.

She sighed and I turned to face her. "Maybe we should go inside. I could quickly check in on Charlie while we wait for them to finish talking," I said.

"That's a good idea." Sophia linked her elbow in mine before dragging me inside. "I'll put the coffee on. I have a feeling it's going to be a long night."

While Sophia headed to the kitchen, I slipped into the bedroom. Caroline was lying on the bed cuddling Charlie. She lifted her head and made to move when I entered.

"Don't get up," I said, not wanting to disturb them. "I'm just popping my head in to check that everything's okay."

Caroline stroked Charlie's head, brushing her blonde hair away from her forehead. "She's a little angel," she said. "She stirred a bit, but went straight back to sleep with a cuddle."

I smiled. "Thank you."

"You're welcome."

"No, seriously. Thank you. I don't know what I would have done without you, Franc, and Sophia over the years."

"There's no need for any of that. The two of you are family. Anything we've done has been done out of love."

"I know, and that's even more cause for thanks." Charlie stirred and Caroline made cooing noises at her and stroked her head again. "I'd better go. I'll come back as soon as I know what's happening."

Caroline nodded, and I left ready to face Caleb with dread forming a rock in my stomach. I found both Caleb and Sophia talking together in the kitchen. She handed him a cup of coffee and poured another as soon as I entered.

"Everything okay?" she mouthed while handing it to me. I smiled and nodded, conveying more than my thanks for the coffee. "I guess it's a bit late for introductions, but just in case, Caleb, this is Sophia. Sophia, Caleb."

"It's good to meet you," Caleb said. "Though the circumstances could have been better."

Sophia laughed. "Your brother, Cane said much the same thing this morning." Caleb smiled at Sophia, while she gave me a quick wink.

"So, this fiancé of yours. I've been talking it through with Tom, and I think it might be a good idea if you do go stay with him, with a couple of the brothers tagging along for protection."

Sophia took a sip of her coffee and gave me a look over the rim of her cup, no doubt wondering where that left the whole business of Caleb not knowing about Charlie. She shouldn't worry, I'd already made my mind up on that front.

I pulled out a chair from the kitchen table and sat before taking a long swig on my coffee. The hot liquid sluiced down my throat and hit my empty stomach, making me realize how hungry I was. I hadn't eaten since breakfast, and that had been before seven this morning. I looked at the clock and noted it was almost ten at night. Strange how much life could change in such a short space of time. You'd think I would have learned that lesson years ago.

"Sophia," I said and placed my cup carefully on the table in front of me. "You, Franc and Caroline should go to Ben's. I don't want to cause you any more trouble and I'm hoping it won't follow you if I'm not around."

Sophia remained quiet, staring into space, which was very unlike her. She could be as stubborn as Caleb at times and the fact she wasn't protesting had me a little worried.

"Can you still send a couple of brothers to watch over them?" I asked Caleb.

"Of course. It's the least I can fucking do." He eyed me with curious relief, as though he knew I'd decided to stay with him but was afraid to jump to say anything for fear I'd change my mind. "Let me just make a call." He stood and pulled his phone out of his pocket. "Cane," he said and walked into the living room while I turned my attention back to Sophia.

"You okay?" I asked because she still had a distant look on her face.

She huffed out a breath and sat at the table opposite me. "You sure, I can't persuade you to come with us?" she asked, and I shook my head. "Didn't think so. What about...?" She raised her eyebrows, but Charlie's name remained unspoken.

I reached over and grabbed her hand. "I'll tell him as soon as he gets off the phone," I whispered.

"Okay." Sophia stared at our hands for a few seconds before pulling away and reaching into the pocket of her robe. "I wasn't sure whether or not to tell you about this," she said and pulled out a piece of paper before putting it on the table.

My stomach churned at the sight of it, even though I didn't know what it was. From the look on Sophia's face, it couldn't be good. "What is it?" I asked.

Sophia glanced through the door at Caleb still talking on the phone and then back at the piece of paper. It sat like a rattlesnake between us.

"It was tied to the rock thrown through the window. I didn't tell the cop about it." She shook her head. "Damn it. Maybe I should have. I don't know what the hell the right thing to do is."

"Telling me and me alone was the right thing." I reached for the paper, my hand shaking, Before I had the chance to pick it up, Caleb slammed his hand down on top of it, and pulled it away.

His face became red and mottled after he unfolded it and read the message it contained. His teeth clenched and the veins on his head damn near popped.

"What does it say?" I asked, but Caleb crunched the paper between his hands and shoved it in his pocket.

"I'm gonna fucking kill him," he said and stormed from the room.

I chased after him and tried to pull him back. "Please," I said. "Caleb. What did it say? Don't do anything stupid." He stopped abruptly and turned to face me, pulling me tight against him, and smashing his lips against mine as though it was the last kiss he'd ever give me. "Please, don't go," I said, when he pulled back, even though he'd left me breathless.

"I have to."

He pulled away and jumped on his bike, speeding down the street as though cops were chasing him.

Sophia stood in the doorway to the bungalow. "What did it say?" I asked, my voice distant to my own ears.

"It said, 'Since last time I fucked your girlfriend didn't draw you out'—" She swallowed heavily and cleared her throat "—'I'll be sure to make the next instance far more fucking eventful. Meet me at Ta-Towhee Bar & Grill. Now.'"

I bent double and tried to take deep breaths to stop myself from throwing up. It took a few seconds, but my worry for Caleb overrode my worry for myself. "Thea," I said. "We have to call Thea."

Sophia ran inside. She was already on the phone and dialing when I joined her. I snatched it from her hands. "Thea," I said as soon as she answered. "It's Amber. I need to speak with Cane."

"He just left," she said. "What's wrong?"

"It's Caleb. He's in trouble."

"Okay. Hang tight. I'll see if I can reach him." With that, she ended the call. I paced the living room, unsure of what to do. A part of me wanted to jump in my car and race after him, but I knew that would only cause more trouble.

"We should call the police officer, Tom," Sophia said.

I looked at her earnest face and knew exactly what she was saying and all that it meant. "Okay," I said.

CHAPTER SIX

Caleb

Ta-Towhee Bar & Grill was off the I-25 close to Woodmoor. The patrons who frequented it had spilled out into the gravel parking lot out front. Most of the men wore denim. I lasered in on the few who sported biker leathers, but none bore the lion's skull insignia of the Feral Sons. The women were dressed in short skirts and cropped tops with an equal mix of leather and denim alike with their drunken chatter filling the night air along with the incessant bass of the music within.

Despite Ta-Towhee's reputation as a dive bar, the wood siding looked like it had been freshly stained and the sign announcing its name gleamed bright red and unblemished in its spotlight, with a newly painted picture of the Towhee bird sitting next to it. It wasn't known as a hang-out for bikers, least of all the fucking Feral Sons. Maybe that's why Leo had chosen it for our meet-up. There was less risk of someone I knew being there to provide a helping hand. Who fucking needed one? I was ready to rip his head off and spit down his throat for what he'd done to Amber.

As I gave a cursory glance to the eight motorcycles parked in the lot, I wondered why the hell Leo had chosen now to act. He'd attacked Amber damn near four fucking years ago. Just the thought of him being near Amber had my hand wringing the handlebars of my bike as though they were Leo's neck. What was he playing at now, and how the fuck did he know she was back in town?

I shook my head and stifled the growl building in my chest. I needed to keep all my rage-fueled energy locked in until I faced the fucker. If Leo wanted to have it out once and for all, then so be it. I didn't need to survive a beating from his brothers, I just needed to make sure I took him out first.

After resisting driving my bike straight through the door and into the building, I pulled to a stop as near as I could to the bar, set my jaw, and allowed all the rage I'd felt over the last four years, all the fucking pain amplified by Amber's revelation, to build like an inferno inside me. Adrenaline rushed through my body and my heartbeat thumped in my ears, but my vision became focused, laser beaming on one task: finding Leo.

The exterior of Ta-Towhee may have had a face-lift, but the

familiar stench of sweat, alcohol, and cigarette smoke filled the renovated interior. Despite the smoking ban for indoor places, it hung in the air over the patrons like a thick, lung-clogging fog that seemed almost alive as lights pulsed to the beat of the music, setting it aglow.

No wonder people were spilling out into the parking lot; the place was fucking packed with people crammed together like sardines, and the noise at a got-to-shout level. I wasted no time barreling through the shifting crowd. Then I spotted him.

Leo.

As a rule, I'd tried to keep my distance from the Feral Sons. Leo was a prick and tried to wind me up, push my buttons, but out of respect for his Dad and the friendship he'd once shared with mine, I'd kept my cool. That cool was all fucking gone now.

It was as though time had slowed and all the other people had faded from my senses. Their voices and the booming music became nothing more than a muffled pressure in my brain. I zoomed in on the only fucker I needed to see.

Leo smirked. His mouth opened, ready to speak, but I wasn't here to waste my time on fucking pleasantries. Besides, there was nothing he had to say that I wished to hear. My fist clenched and slammed into his face with a satisfying crunch that I felt more than heard. His head flew backward, and I laid into him again, grabbing him by the T-shirt and tugging him close to stop him from falling to the ground.

The vague notion that a woman screamed close by flashed through my mind, and then another. The crush moved away and the space around us opened. Even with the blood dripping from Leo's nose, and the cut on his lip, he still looked at me with mocking eyes.

I pitched to the side, losing my grip on him. Someone had barreled into me. Two fuckers tried to grab my arms, but I swung them together. They clunked heads before falling back. A sudden gush of sharp pain lanced up into my guts as some fucker speared me in the back with a kidney shot. I sucked in a harsh breath. It hurt like a motherfucker but didn't bring me down. Besides, from experience, I knew it wasn't hard enough to see me pissing blood for a week. The fucker who blindsided me was too much of a pussy to land a blow like that.

I fought off fucker after fucker. My muscles tightened under the strain. Blow after blow landed on me, but a strange numbness stopped me from feeling them. I tried to keep my eye on my goal, but Leo pulled back, leaving the bar, and leaving his brothers to deal with me. The fucking coward was too much of a pussy to take me on himself.

My knee buckled under an unseen blow to the back of my leg. I fell to the floor, crashing. With Leo's departure, my senses clicked back on as though someone had flipped a switch. My face felt as though someone had hit me with a brick ten times, and my ribs didn't feel much better. All the fight rushed from me like water down an unplugged drain. Once again, I'd failed Amber.

Time slowed again. Nothing mattered anymore. My only hope was that Cane would reach her and keep her safe.

At that thought, an image of my brother swirled into view. He speared the fucker in front of me with a punch to the head. Other voices shouted and footsteps pounded, but the noise was hollow and distant to my ears.

Cane grabbed me by the arm and pulled me to my feet. I was surrounded by several of my brothers from Forever Midnight. The last of the Feral Sons had fled as my back-up arrived.

"What the fuck were you thinking?" Cane asked.

I guess that was the problem. I wasn't fucking thinking. "Amber." Just saying her name had pain lancing through my jaw.

"She's fine. You're lucky she fucking called." Cane shook his head and pulled me through the bar to the exit.

CHAPTER SEVEN

Amber

"No. Don't want to." Charlie kicked her heels against the kitchen counter she sat atop.

"We have to, baby," I said. "The window is all smashed and we have to leave the house while the repair men come and fix it right up."

"Go with Aunt Caroline."

I huffed out a breath. Knowing how hard and confusing this was for me, it had to be a million times more so for her, and my worry and unease wasn't making her mood any better.

Caroline brushed Charlie's hair behind her ear and stroked her cheek. "There's not enough room at Ben's for us all to stay. But we'll see you at the wedding in a few days." She lifted Charlie's teddy bear from the counter, waved it in Charlie's face, and pretended it was speaking.

"I'm coming with you," Teddy said in a voice made to imitate that of Yogi Bear. "You can cuddle me and talk to me and have picnics with me. We'll have lots of adventures to share with everyone." With that, Caroline bopped Charlie on the nose with the teddy.

Charlie kicked the counter again, but this time giggled as she did so. She pulled the bear in for a hug but gave Lucky a weary look out of the corner of her eye.

The few minutes we'd waited for Thea to call back had been the longest of my life, and the relief I felt when the phone rang and I answered to find that she had caught up with Cane made me light-headed.

Thea had given him Sophia's number so he could save time and speak to me directly. As soon as I explained the situation, he told me to hang tight, and that he'd send Lucky and a few other brothers to pick me up and take the Cortezes to Ben's. From the look on Lucky's face when he arrived and learned that Charlie would be coming with me, Cane hadn't fully briefed him on my situation.

Sophia carried two garment bags into the kitchen and draped them over the back of a dining chair. "You'll need these for the wedding," she said, and gave me a tight smile. She knew I'd do all I could to make it, but no guarantees were on the table.

"I guess that's everything," I said.

"Yep."

Caroline picked Charlie up and gave her a big hug. Franc pecked her on the cheek and pretended to steal her nose.

"What? You need this?" he said while sticking the tip of his thumb between his knuckled fingers. "I'd better put it back then." He did so with a popping sound.

Charlie laughed and a wave of love washed through me for our adopted family. I shook back the tears forming in my eyes for fear of Charlie seeing them and gave both Franc and Sophia a hug.

"Call me in the morning with an update," Sophia said.

"Of course." I scooped Caroline in a hug with Charlie, and she kissed me on the cheek.

"Take care and call us if you need anything," she said.

I gave her a wry smile and transferred Charlie into my arms before walking over to the chair and picking up the garment bags and looking at Lucky.

"We'll all leave at the same time." He picked up my cases still unpacked after our arrival this morning.

Within minutes we were bidding a second goodbye outside. Sophia and her parents jumped into their car with a couple of brothers from Forever Midnight following on their bikes behind them.

Charlie and I jumped in a car with Lucky, and another couple of brothers followed us. Before we'd gone two blocks, my phone rang.

"Caleb," I said, hoping it was him.

"It's Officer Tom Davenport. Caleb's fine." He huffed a breath along the line. "He's alive at any rate. A team of paramedics is looking him over. He's got some questions to answer and then I'll let him go."

My head was too full of the fact Caleb had been injured to process much of what he said, but I clung to the fact that Caleb was also alive.

Earlier, while I'd been busy telling Cane to get to Ta-Towhee, Sophia had been on the other line telling Tom the same thing, and my resolve to file a police report as soon as possible had settled around my heart. It seemed strange to say it, but although the fear of that night would always be locked inside me, telling Caleb had in many ways made it easier to bear. I would always hold the memory of what happened but felt now that it was in the background - one night in a long list of experiences that defined me. Maybe telling the police would help keep it there. Hell, if I had gone to the police and told them what happened all those years ago, maybe it would have happened sooner. Leo would be behind bars and Caleb wouldn't have risked his life or the possibility of prison himself by going after him.

"Thank you for letting me know," I said, and shook the

thought from my mind. Life was full of regrets. I knew the only thing to do was accept the mistakes you made and try to learn from them, but that was easier said than done.

~

After all the excitement, the ride to the safe house had lulled Charlie back to sleep. I cradled her in my arms and lifted her from the car ready to carry inside.

It felt strange to have Lucky and the other brothers with me. Like I'd stepped back in time to a different life. I'd stayed away from the whole biker scene in order to keep my location a secret. Not that I'd ever been a big part of it anyway.

A slight smile played on my lips as I remembered how Caleb and I met. He'd been passing through the airport on a business trip with his dad. Terminal security had stopped them as they tried to enter the first-class lounge. They weren't exactly the kind of clientele we were used to having. After they'd shown their passes and were allowed to enter, I did my job and tried to offer them the service all our guests expected. Not an easy thing to do when Caleb looked at me as though trying to burn through my soul. His dad nudged his arm and told him it was rude to stare, making me blush further, but Caleb grumbled something in return and continued eyeballing me. His gaze set me on edge but stirred something inside at the same time.

"Another business trip?" I asked a few days later when he returned to the lounge without his father.

"No. This one's all pleasure." He handed me a ticket and when I checked, it had my name on it. He looked at his phone. "Seeing as you finish work in five minutes, I thought you could accompany me."

Creepy stalker behavior aside, I said yes. The rest, as they say, is history. I'm not going to pretend it was love at first sight, more like lust mixed with a little fear, but that soon turned to love. Caleb was a lot of things. He could be intimidating to others, though never to me after our first meeting. He was intense and quick to anger. Not to mention insatiable in bed. But he was also one of the most caring people I had ever met and would do anything for those he considered family.

And I'd left him.

I hefted Charlie in my arms, shifting her to a more comfortable position. The safe house, as Lucky called it, was a colonial farmhouse set amongst a few acres of land. The lights were on, and a pick-up truck was parked in the secluded driveway. As soon as I stepped inside, Thea rushed towards me. She stopped a foot or so away as though suddenly aware we barely knew each other.

"Let's get the little one into bed," she said, making me grateful she was careful not to mention Charlie's name in front of Lucky, even though that ship had sailed at the Cortezes' house.

I could wish that I'd told Caleb about her before the other brothers had a chance to make assumptions themselves, but wishes are as good as a fork when all you have to eat is soup.

Thea guided me upstairs and into a bedroom, where she pulled back the covers and I laid Charlie in the bed. I sat beside Charlie for a few seconds, staring at her perfect, tiny face. When I stood, I tucked Teddy into her arms and placed pillows either side of her to stop her from rolling onto the floor in the unfamiliar bed.

"You should get some rest too," Thea said.

"I won't be able to sleep."

"You might surprise yourself."

I stood and took her hand, squeezing it and smiling. "Thank you for helping." The words were almost drowned out by the rumble from my stomach.

"Let's grab something to eat. I'm famished," she said and pulled me from the room.

Thea looked very much at home in the large, open-plan kitchen with more cupboard and floor space than anyone could ever need. She set to work making us both some food, and I felt guilty letting her, but she refused my help when offered.

"How long have you and Caleb been together?" I asked as I sat on a breakfast bar stool, next to the kitchen island, and watched her get to work.

"Ten months," she answered and patted her baby-bump.

"He's different to how I remember him. You must make him very happy."

"He makes me very happy too." Thea unhooked a griddle from a rack above our heads and set it to heat on the stove before building up a cheese sandwich, buttering both sides of the bread. When it was ready, she placed it on the griddle. "Did you get a chance to talk to Caleb?" she asked.

"I told him what happened, but not about Charlie." I sighed. "I was going to. It's just, things happened..." I choked back a sob and rubbed my hand over my head. Caleb was alive. It didn't matter that he needed a paramedic. He was alive. "I-I don't even know what state Caleb's in. How much he's hurt."

Thea flipped the grilled cheese onto a plate and rushed to my side. "He's fine. Those cotton heads. I can't believe they didn't call you."

"They don't have my number," I said, realizing that while Cane had Sophia's, I'd never given either of them mine.

"Still, they could have found a way to let you know through Lucky." She pulled the plate toward me, told me to eat, and edged back around the center island to make another sandwich for herself. "Cane said that he's battered and bruised but he is far too thick-headed for there to be any lasting damage."

I smiled. Cane sounded a lot politer than I remembered, and I was certain Thea had left out an expletive or two.

Thea huffed out a breath and plated her food before taking the stool next to mine. "He also said that they arrived just in time. Eight of the Feral Sons were laying into him. He didn't stand a chance by himself, no matter how strong or skilled he is. The Landon's are both as pig-headed as each other. I don't know what he was thinking. One man can't beat eight in a fistfight." She took a bite of her sandwich and murmured appreciatively. "I really was famished," she said before taking another. "I swear this baby needs feeding every twenty minutes."

With my own stomach starved of food, I cleared my plate in moments, beating Thea to the punch. "I just wish they were back already," I said as soon as I swallowed the last morsel.

"Hopefully, they won't be much longer."

I stared at the ceiling and the rose-colored pots and pans hanging from a rack above the island. "Your home is lovely," I said. "I never thought I'd see the day Cane moved out of his cabin. Although I guess with a baby on the way you could use more space."

Thea chuckled. "He hasn't changed that much since you knew him. We're still in the cabin, although it's undergone some renovations in the last few months." She waved her hand around the room. "This belongs to someone Jameson knows in New

York. They use it as a holiday rental. He suggested it to Cane as a place you could hide out without anyone suspecting we were here."

"Jameson must know some fancy people."

"I guess. He's not much of a talker, so I wouldn't know."

"Nothing's changed there then." I lifted the plate from in front of Thea, and despite her protests, I insisted I would do the washing up. Now that I knew this wasn't her house, there was no way I was letting her wait on me.

"You know," she said after a moment. "Cane also mentioned one other thing about Caleb when he called."

"He did?"

"He said that the first thing he did when Cane got to him was ask after you."

There was nothing I could say to that, so I didn't try. It was obvious from our meeting this afternoon that Caleb still had feelings for me, and no matter how hard I'd tried to deny them over the years, I had feelings for him too.

I finished the dishes and put them away in the places I'd watched Thea grab them from. I was about to suggest we head upstairs and get some sleep when a car sounded outside. I rushed to the hallway and saw lights flash through the window before going dim.

My heart thundered. The lights hadn't belonged to a

motorcycle. Lucky was out of one of the front rooms and at the door before I had the chance to think straight. When he opened it, I held my breath. After far too long, he flung it wide.

"What the fuck happened to you?" he said. "You look like you rode your bike head on into a tank."

"Fucking feels like it," Caleb answered and stepped inside.

CHAPTER EIGHT

Amber

In the light of the hallway, the bruises on his face stood out like bright red welts. His lip was cracked and swollen, and from the way he clutched his stomach, I knew he must have damaged some ribs.

I'd be heartbroken if I wasn't so furious. I stormed up to him and almost slapped him across the face myself. "Is this how things are going to be? Don't you realize this is the main reason I left in the first damn place?" My voice reached octaves so high, I was certain the glass in the windows would shatter. "I can't believe you could be this stupid." I threw my hands in the air and turned to leave, deciding the best thing to do was get him out of my sight.

"Amber."

I stopped on the stairs with my back to him. "No," I said over my shoulder. "Don't you dare speak my name as though you care one iota what I think or feel? If you did, you would never have gone to that stupid bar."

"Just calm down."

That was it. If he thought I was mad a moment ago, he was in for a shock. In our years apart, he'd grown stupid. His brain power had no doubt diminished with all the steroids he'd taken to achieve his bulk. At that moment in time, it didn't matter that I knew he would never do such a thing.

I turned on the stairs and faced him again. Cane stood behind Caleb. Only when Thea moved alongside them and lifted her chin and motioned her eyes upstairs did I consider that any more shouting would wake Charlie. For a moment, my frustration and anger had overridden my senses. Although I was prepared to tell Caleb everything, I wasn't about to do so this second.

I huffed out a breath, walked back down the few steps I'd taken, and pushed past Caleb into the night air with the intention of walking around the house a couple of times to dissipate my anger.

The wind howled. Despite the warmth of the day, the night was decidedly chilly. I wrapped my arms tightly around myself and cursed.

How could I have been so stupid to bring Charlie here?

Yeah, great plan. For the first time, I almost wished Caleb wasn't her father. Not that I knew either way. Then she wouldn't have her first meeting with him looking like — how did Lucky put it? — like he rode his bike straight into a tank.

"What the hell is wrong with you, Amber?" Caleb called as he followed behind me. "What did you expect me to do, sit and wait for Leo to fucking rape you again?"

Tears welled in my eyes. I continued stomping around the house, placing one foot in front of the other.

"Fuck! I'm sorry. I'm such a fucking asshole." He placed his hand on my arm and pulled me to a stop.

"You're always a fucking asshole. I can't have that part of you in my life. Not now."

Not knowing what I meant, he huffed out a sigh and looked to his feet. "Don't go. Don't… fucking run away from me again."

"Don't you see? I ran away to stop this from happening." I waved my hand and gestured towards his face. "Or worse. Tell me, what would have happened if Cane hadn't come to the bar? What if Thea hadn't been able to reach him straight away and I would have had to wait for him to arrive at Sophia's house? How long would it have taken for him to reach you? Thirty… forty minutes? Where would you be right fucking now if Cane had turned up more than half an hour later?"

"I'd have managed."

"Yeah, your face tells me how well you would have managed." I poked him in the ribs and shook my head when he winced. "Yeah, you'd have been fucking fine."

Without waiting for a reply, I pulled out of his grasp and continued pacing around the house. I ignored the thoughts bombarding my mind and the biting wind that made my face burn and pulled the leaves from the trees, causing them to swirl around me. Caleb followed a few steps behind. Anger, frustration, and increasing worry for what might have been fueled my steps.

When I'd completed a full circle of the house and was about to start another, he sped up and pulled me to a stop again. "You're going to make yourself sick if you don't go inside and get warm."

"I'm not making you stay with me. If you're worried for yourself, go inside."

"Amber, please. Be angry at me all you want, just do it fucking inside." His voice rose on the final words, and I knew if I didn't do as he asked, he would likely pick me up and carry me in.

"Fine, but only because I fucking want to." My words sounded childish to my own ears, but I couldn't help them.

I returned inside and headed through the first downstairs doorway I came to. He'd likely follow me upstairs and wake Charlie. I'd half expected to find Lucky inside, as it was the room he'd emerged from earlier, but instead, I found a living room. Two couches sat facing each other, and a floor lamp set the room in a warm orange glow. Caleb closed the door, sealing us in the room together.

I sat on one of the couches, but when Caleb sat next to me, I stood and moved to the other. My gaze landed on his battered face and saw the smirk on it. It widened. I tried to look away but could feel it burning into the side of my face.

Damn it! I hated it when he did this. He always fucking knew that if he grinned at me continuously, eventually, I'd crack and smile back. Not this time. I stood and turned to face the windows, but the curtains were drawn, and I felt like an idiot staring at their fleur-de-lis pattern. Still, he grinned. I just knew it.

"This is not fucking funny," I said and turned to face him.

He kept on grinning. "Then why are you smiling?" he said and stood before walking toward me.

"I'm not." As I said the words, my face cracked under his onslaught, and I smiled.

I desperately wanted to stay angry at him. But a huge grin split his face, and he leaned forward, giving me a tentative kiss on the lips, as though testing both my willingness to be kissed and the pain he might feel in the action. Obviously deciding both were acceptable, he deepened his kiss.

My legs trembled, and I felt as though all the air had been sucked from the room. With each kiss, each flick of his tongue against my own, my anger diminished, shifting from hard stone into something far more soft and squishy. In an attempt to regain my control of the situation, I pulled away. "It's really not funny," I said, unable to look him in the eye. "You could have been killed."

He cupped my face in his hands and lifted my head to look at him. "I'm sorry. I promised you earlier that I wouldn't go off half-cocked, but when I saw that fucking letter that's exactly what I did. It won't happen again."

"Yes, it will. You can't help yourself."

He lifted my chin higher and kissed me again. Worried where things might lead and that I might hurt him, I pulled away. "We shouldn't." It seemed as though I was always saying those words before we did exactly what we shouldn't do.

"You didn't seem to mind earlier in the shower."

"Who the hell does that?" I growled and shook my head. "There I was minding my own business—"

Another grin split Caleb's face, halting my flow. He raised an eyebrow, and I remembered exactly what *business* I'd been about when he interrupted my shower.

He ran his finger along my chin and brushed the tip over my lips.

My heart skipped a beat. I swallowed, trying to alleviate the dryness in my throat. Caleb licked his lips, and I wanted nothing more than to bite them. "I could hurt you," I said.

"I'll take my chances." He inched forward and pressed his knee between my legs.

I tried to say something, but the words were lost when Caleb pressed his soft lips against my own. My head spun, and this time, my body responded with desperate need. I opened my mouth and welcomed his tongue. His kiss was deep and demanding. I gasped and pulled him closer, backing towards the couch. I wanted Caleb Landon with every fiber of my being. I always had. I wanted to latch onto him and never let him go.

Trails of need ignited my core. Caleb drove me out of my mind with worry and crazy with desire, but I realized, no matter what, I could never leave him again.

He reached down, lifted the T-shirt I'd borrowed from him earlier over my head, and tossed it aside. My bra was quick to follow. My jeans and panties were not long after that. He pushed against me, his hard cock straining through his jeans and against my belly.

I gasped, and he stepped back to look at me before taking my breasts in his hands. "You are so beautiful, and these are fucking amazing.

I blushed. It had been a long time since anyone had made me

feel pretty. I guessed being a single mom had made me feel as though that part of my life was over. Caleb grinned like a kid in a candy shop, licked his lips, and circled my hard nipples between his thumbs and forefingers, sending shockwaves shooting up my spine. The room spun as sensations swirled within me.

A melting desire, only ever brought on by Caleb, threatened to turn me into a puddle of molten liquid. I reached for his T-shirt and undressed him in much the same way he'd undressed me. I tried not to focus on the evidence of his beating displayed in full screaming color across his skin and kept my gaze firmly moving from his deep brown eyes to his exquisite cock, trusting that he would stop our actions if the pain of his injuries became too much to bear.

He grabbed my ass, lifted me from the floor, and deposited me on the couch.

I laughed. "Well, this is an interesting development," I said, echoing his earlier words.

His face brightened, and his eyes roamed over every inch of me. He spread my legs apart before lowering his head between my thighs, even though all I wanted was to be fucked. I smiled and hoped he'd make me beg.

"You are so fucking perfect. I've always known you were made for me."

I wanted to protest his cocksure attitude, but the words died on the tip of my tongue as he moved his up and down, tasting my free-slowing juices. His tongue darted inside, delving deeper into my core. I shook with need as he flicked my clit with his fingers before they switched places with his tongue. They plunged inside while his mouth found my throbbing nub. His free hand ran over my stomach and pressed me into the couch, while his fingers pounded into me, and his mouth worked my clit into a pulsing fireball.

"I need you in me, Caleb," I said. "I need you to fuck me."

"All in good fucking time."

I almost howled in frustration, but Caleb continued to work. I bit my lip and groaned, wriggling my body, desperate to get what I needed. My core tightened around his fingers, as his lips closed around my clit again, sucking me in as though I was the tastiest of lollipops. His fingers and tongue worked in unison, building a rhythm of desire that rocked my body.

I grabbed his head and pushed him down, wanting, needing more. My breaths came fast and hard. Heat built inside and my eyes rolled in my head, but when I was just about to climax, he withdrew, leaving me bereft.

"You fucking asshole," I said.

"It's why you love me."

I growled, jumped on all fours on the couch and grabbed his cock, squeezing it between my hands and pulling him closer.

The need within me built to a palpable urgency. I licked my lips, remembering how delicious he'd tasted in the shower. His eyes closed, and his head fell back when I flicked out my tongue and licked the glistening precum from his tip.

I ran my tongue up and down his thick shaft and moaned as I sucked him into my mouth. The tip of his cock hit the back of my throat, I almost gagged on his size, but still craved more. I slid my head back and forth, allowing his hardness to fill my mouth. I loved the sensation of having him inside me, of teasing him with my mouth and tongue while cupping his balls and squeezing them in my hands. The thought of him pumping his seed into my mouth sent a rush of pleasure to my core and made me work faster. I wanted to please him, to taste his salty goodness.

He thrust into my mouth and then groaned before his finger threaded my hair and pulled me back. My wetness dribbled down my leg.

Caleb looked at me with that devilish grin of his. His gaze filled with lust. I softly brushed the velvet head of his cock with my lips and shuddered at my need to taste the sweet nectar of his seed.

"Bend forward over the arm of the couch," he said.

I did. My heart raced, and my core pulsed in excitement.

His fingers followed my spine, trailing down my back and

over the curve of my bottom. I gasped as they probed the wet silken flesh of my folds, teasing my entrance before pushing inside.

A shiver ran through me. Caleb plunged his fingers deeper into my core while he circled my throbbing clit. I wanted to rock my hips in time to his penetrating fingers, to squirm and lift to meet them, but he pinned me to the arm of the couch. I buried my head in the material to keep from crying out in a mixture of pleasure and frustration.

He withdrew his fingers and circled my clit in slow, soft movements. From behind, Caleb spread my legs wide and dipped his head. His warm breath between my cheeks caused a tremor to run over my body. A tentative tongue swiped at my folds. I whimpered, and Caleb let out a satisfied moan. His hand reached around my body and found my breast. He tweaked and pinched my nipple as his tongue circled my clit and made long, sure strokes along my slit.

I panted, wanting, needing more, but I knew he would deny me if I tried to take it. All I could do was bury my face in the arm of the chair and keep my ass in the air while Caleb teased me with his mouth and his fingers.

The ache inside of me built. I panted. "Oh, fuck, Caleb." Vibrations raced inside me, and my core tightened around his fingers. Wetness streamed from me, but I held back for fear my climax would end our time together.

My breathing quickened. I needed to arch my back, to come. "I can't," I gasped. "Please."

In an instant, Caleb flipped me and pulled me to my feet. He fell backward onto the couch and pulled me with him. "Mount me," he said and positioned me above his cock.

I was lost in a sea of desire, but kept my movements slow, sliding onto him an inch at a time. I groaned as he speared my body, stretching me open and sliding deeper and deeper inside. Despite my wetness, my tight core had to expand and yield to his width. "Oh, fuck."

"Fucking right, oh, fuck!" His dick throbbed, and my muscles pulsed around him. He grabbed my hips and pulled me down onto him.

I trembled in pleasure as he filled me in a way, I barely remembered was possible. My body rocked over his, and I moaned.

He rose and pushed, and I relished the glide of his cock as we found a steady rhythm.

"You feel so fucking good." Caleb cupped my breasts in his hands, massaging them, caressing my skin. "I'm not gonna make you beg to come." My breath hitched and a flash of disappointment welled, but he continued, "I'm gonna make you beg to stop coming."

I smiled, loving the sight of his hard body. I tried not to think of the bruises that marred his face and body and concentrated on the feeling of him inside me; the sound of his voice as he said the most delicious things.

He guided my hand to my clit and grabbed my hips, pulling me onto him. His bulging cock filled me deeper and deeper, as my fingers circled my nub. "Fuck, you're amazing," he said.

He looked into my eyes. I writhed my hips and spiraled towards orgasm, coming undone. Caleb thrust up into me, building on our friction with the force I needed. I imploded in a climax so intense my nerve endings overloaded, and I thought I'd pass out. Caleb didn't let up, he flipped us around and withdrew, dropping to kneel on the floor, down to my folds and meeting them with his mouth. He licked at my slit, lapping up my juices and sucking my clit into his mouth, drawing out my orgasm until I couldn't breathe.

I gasped, sucking in air. The flood of sensation made my vision go black. I screamed, unable to take any more. Sweat glistened on my body. I drifted on a haze of pleasure for a moment, before sobering. "You didn't come," I said as a smile played on the edge of my lips. I knew what that meant.

Caleb lifted his head and quirked an eyebrow. He nipped the inside of my thigh before peppering a trail of kisses up my body, tickling me with his breath in the process.

"That's because I said I'd make you beg to stop coming," he said before kissing me hard.

I tasted myself on his lips and gasped when he teased my entrance with the tip of his cock.

CHAPTER NINE

Caleb

This time with Amber was fucking everything. I would have stayed an eternity in our weird little bubble of the living room, but when she rested her head against my chest and stared at the wall, I felt her tension growing.

"Everything will be fine," I said and trailed my hand over her shoulder. "Leo won't find you here."

Amber rolled and propped her head on her hands to look at me. "You're still going to go after him, aren't you?" she asked and ran her fingers over a bruise around my eye, making me wince. "What if I said I didn't want you to?"

"I can't stand by and do fucking nothing."

"I'm not asking you to." She sat up and pulled the cushion from the back of the couch, tugging it to her breasts, drawing her knees close, and wrapping her arms around both of them. "I've decided to speak to Tom and file a police report. Maybe he can arrest Leo. We should try to follow the law, at least at first."

I looked at the floor unsure what to say. My insides raged and I wanted nothing more than to smash Leo's fucking face in with my fists, but I knew how difficult it was for Amber to deal with that side of my personality. She'd as good as told me that she couldn't have that part of me in her life, and I didn't want to risk pushing her away when I'd just got her back.

"If that's what you want, I'll do it," I said although the vein in my head popped at the thought. "But it won't be easy. They may take Leo in for questioning, but any evidence will be long gone."

Her eyes darted to the door and I wondered for a second if she'd heard someone coming when I hadn't. I held my breath, listening, but no one was there.

"Let's grab our clothes and talk about this upstairs where no one can interrupt us," I said and moved to stand.

Amber tugged on my arm and pulled me back down.

"There's something you need to know." The tone in her voice made my jaw clench. What the fuck could be worse than what she'd already been through?

I edged closer to her. When she remained silent and stared at the door again, I had to stifle the growl building inside me. Not two minutes ago she'd made me agree to let the law deal with Leo, and now I just knew there was more to this fucking story.

More hurt he had caused than she'd already told.

I clasped onto her hand and squeezed. "What is it, Amber?"

She shifted her gaze from the door and looked at me for a long moment. When she finally spoke, her voice was deadpan. "A month or so after I left, I found out I was pregnant."

Fuck!

Not only had she dealt with her attack all by herself, but she'd also had to deal with the aftermath too. Fucking Leo. If it wasn't for my agreement with Amber, I'd do more than kill him.

She had always wanted kids. We'd even talked about having them together — another reason her leaving struck me so hard. For her to have to deal with a pregnancy under the circumstances must have been fucking devastating.

I was about to ask if she had been able to rely on her friend to accompany her for an abortion, when I realized she was staring at the door again, or rather, at something beyond the door.

"You had the kid," I said after clearing my throat. She only nodded in response. "Is he here in this house?"

"She. She's here in this house, asleep upstairs."

I huffed out a breath and found myself also staring at the fucking door.

"She's brave and funny," Amber continued, "and so caring. When she looks at me, I know that no matter what happened, I have my baby girl, and she's worth more than anything I could ever ask for."

I stiffened on the couch. After a moment, I grabbed my jeans and pulled them on. My jaw set. A tightness formed in my chest, and I suddenly felt too hot to be inside. That fucking wind howling through the window seemed like the kick I needed to my senses right now, and I considered going outside to let it blast in my face.

Wordlessly, I handed Amber her clothes, trying to order the feelings welling inside me. "Is she Leo's?" I asked.

Amber choked back a sob. "Does it matter?"

As she said the words everything I'd been feeling clicked into place: resolve, determination, love.

I shook my head. "If she's brave, funny, and caring then she's nothing to do with Leo." I tugged on my T-shirt and straightened it down. "Fuck," I said. "I'm way too much of a fucking mess to meet my daughter with all these bruises. What the fuck is she going to think?"

Amber leaped to her feet, dropping her clothes to the floor in the process, and flung her arms around my neck. Tears streamed down her face, and she buried her head against my chest.

I laughed. "Now on top of everything fucking else, I'm gonna have your snot on my top."

Amber laughed and rubbed her head against my chest even more. "You're gonna be perfect," she said after she'd pulled back.

"Just mind your language. I'll not have our daughter growing up with a gutter tongue like you and your brother."

My heart swelled at her words, *our daughter*. I had a fucki— I had a daughter.

Amber grabbed my hand. "Let's go see her," she said and tugged me toward the exit. "We'll just pop our heads around the bedroom door. If she stirs, we can talk to her, but otherwise, it might be best to speak to her in the morning."

"That sounds perfect. I'd love to." I grinned and pulled her back for a quick kiss, sealing her lips with my own. When I lifted my head, I kept her tight in my arms and raised an eyebrow. "I may be a complete mess," I said. "But if she does wake up, at least I'm dressed."

I laughed when Amber's eyes darted downward and her mouth gaped as she realized she was still naked. She pushed me back and gave me a scowl as though that was my fault before grabbing her clothes from the floor and throwing them on. "She's going to have a million questions as it is. We don't need to add why I'm naked to the pile of them." After she'd finished dressing, she smoothed her clothes down her body, huffed out a breath, and looked me in the eyes. "Her name is Charlie," she said, and my heart damn near fucking swelled to the size of the Empire State building.

I held my hand out for her to grab. "Let's go see Charlie," I said.

CHAPTER TEN

Amber

I could barely process Caleb's reaction to learning about Charlie. In many ways, it was a huge relief, more than I could have ever expected. But with that relief came another huge dose of regret. I'd denied not only Caleb, but me and Charlie, the life we should have been living for far too long.

She didn't stir when we popped our heads around the door to look at her. Caleb stood staring at her without saying a word. Eventually, I dragged him from the room, saying that we needed to get some sleep while there was still time.

"You should stay with her," he said, and for a second, my chest tightened with worry that he'd had a change of heart about the whole situation, but he continued, "If she wakes up in a strange place without you near, she might be frightened."

"You're probably right. She was asleep when I put her to bed, so nothing here is familiar to her."

He pulled me into his arms and held me tight. I sensed the worry churning through his thoughts.

"What's wrong?" I asked.

He huffed out a breath and held me tighter, resting his cheek on the top of my head. "Do you think she'll like me? I've not had much experience with small children. Besides the bruises, what if she's scared of my size, or my tattoos? What if I frighten her?"

Despite myself, I laughed. It wasn't that Caleb's appearance wasn't intimidating. I'd seen grown-ass men cross the street to avoid walking past him. And I'd been worried about the bruises myself, but I realized how silly all that was now. Unless a child had been taught to hate or fear, they had a natural ability to accept everyone they perceived as good. "She's gonna love you," I said. "Do you know what she did when she met Cane?"

"She met Cane?" His voice was strained, and another pang of guilt hit me. He shouldn't have learned about Charlie before Caleb.

"I'm sorry, he knew about Charlie first," I said, worried that I had added to his hurt. "Don't be angry with Cane though, I asked Thea to make him promise to give me a chance to tell you about her before he told you himself."

"I'm not angry at Cane or you. It does explain why he was insistent that I speak to you though." He kissed my forehead. "I could wish for things to have been different. But the past is the past and we can't change that. I'm just happy that you're both here."

"Me too." I leaned up, wrapped my arms around his neck, and planted a soft kiss on his lips.

"I would like to know what she did with Cane though."

I laughed again. It was funny to think of him being afraid of a three-year-old. "She declared that she was a big girl and that she wanted to have her body painted."

"Well, that's easy to arrange."

I pulled back and slapped him on the arm, and then did it again after a big grin split his face. "That's not even funny. Now go. I need to get my beauty sleep and so do you."

"Nah." He lifted his head and stroked his chin. "This mug couldn't get any prettier."

I sighed. I'd missed this so much. "See you in the morning," I said, wishing for all the world I could stay with him, but he was right, Charlie needed me with her.

"In the morning," he said.

~

I gnawed at my lips and stared at my reflection in the mirror. With the bright sunshine shining in the window and the billowing wind of the night before a thing of the past, I'd donned a summer dress with spaghetti straps and a rose pattern. I'd even put on make-up, something I hadn't bothered with in a while, and pulled my hair back in a wispy bun. I'd put Charlie in a cute cotton, racerback dress with a sunflower print. I wanted everything to be perfect, but I'm not sure what that even meant. The butterflies in my stomach made me nauseous, and Charlie was getting restless and wanted to leave the bedroom.

Although I'd reassured Caleb last night that Charlie would love him, worry had set in as I tried to sleep. There was always the possibility I would be wrong. There was even the possibility that Caleb had thought things through himself and had decided that taking on the responsibility of a child was a big ask, especially when that child might not be his. And then there was the question of our relationship. It was easy to be in his presence and know I wanted to stay there forever, but were we really just picking things up where they left off? Too much had happened for that.

I reached for my phone and called Sophia to check in and tell her I was fine and for a bit of advice.

"I don't know Caleb at all," she said as soon as I mentioned my worries. It was easy for me to forget that she'd only met him for the first time yesterday. "But I trust Thea when she says that he still loves you, and if he looks at you anything like his brother looks at Thea, then I think you're good. Besides, nothing you've ever said about him would make me think he'd change his mind about something like this. You always said family was everything to him and that included all the members of Forever Midnight. Not all of them are blood related, so maybe that's not what family means to him." She snorted a faint giggle over the line. "Listen to me all wise and knowing, chica. But trust me, I think Caleb and Charlie are one thing you don't have to worry about right now."

"You're right," I said.

"You bet your sweet behind I am. Now you just focus on staying safe and letting Caleb sort all this mess out so you can make it to my wedding. I don't know what I'd do without my best friend by my side."

"I'll do that," I said and ended the call.

I looked at myself in the mirror again, huffed, and shook my head. Sophia was probably right. Besides, the worst thing that could happen was for Caleb to send us away. If that happened, things would be no different than they were the day before yesterday. At least, that's what I tried to tell myself.

I dragged myself away from the mirror and called Charlie over to the bed, pulling her up onto my lap when she got there.

"There might be some new people downstairs," I said.

"Aunt Caroline, Aunt Sophia, and Uncle Franc too?"

"No. They won't be there. But do you remember Aunt

Sophia's friend, Thea, and her friend Cane, the one with the pictures on his body?"

Charlie pulled Teddy tight against her chest. "He made Mommy sad."

I smiled and kissed her forehead. It was easy to forget how children notice everything. "He didn't make Mommy sad," I said and pushed down the nerves tightening my chest. "You remember how I told you all about Mommy's old friend? The one who used to take her on rides on his motorcycle?"

"Yes. Motorcycle." She bounced up and down on my lap. She loved my stories about Caleb, especially the idea of riding on his bike.

"Well, Cane is his brother, and I was surprised to see him, that's all." I lifted her down from my lap and held her hand. "Cane might be downstairs, and his brother too. Isn't that exciting? Would you like to meet him?"

Charlie nodded, pulled her hand from mine, and ran to the door. I laughed and caught up with her, taking hold of her hand again. A part of me wondered if I should have told her he was her Daddy, but what if he had changed his mind? Where would she be then?

I sighed, plastered a smile on my face, and went downstairs with Charlie. As voices and other sounds came from the kitchen, that's where we headed.

The sweet scent of apple and cinnamon hit me and made my stomach rumble as soon as we stepped through the door.

I spotted Thea, pulling a batch of muffins from the oven. "Good morning," she said and nodded her head toward the doors, leading outside.

"Morning. Those smell delicious."

"Breakfast muffins," she said as she put them on a cooling rack.

Charlie raced toward her. "Charlie want one, please."

Thea crouched down to her level, an act I was more than impressed with given the size of her pregnancy-belly. "Charlie can have one. But I'm sorry, we have to wait a little while until they are cool enough to eat. Okay?"

"Okay." With that, Charlie scanned the rest of the room. My heart damn near stopped when she spotted the doorway, and I saw Cane outside. She didn't hesitate in running toward him.

I followed, racing to catch up with where she was headed. As soon as I stepped outside, I noted Caleb sitting on a wall that surrounded a raised flower display in the garden.

Charlie had spotted him too, and made a beeline for his location, stopping only when she was right up close.

A wide smile lit Caleb's face and he leaned over to talk to her. Before he had the chance to say anything, Charlie tugged on his hand and tried to pull him to his feet.

"Want ride on your motorcycle," she said while grunting with effort.

"You're too little to ride on my motorcycle." Caleb lifted her in his arms and nodded toward me. "But maybe if we talk to your mom, she'll let you sit on one for a little while."

She bounced in his arms. "Yay. Sit on motorcycle."

"Excuse me, young lady." I placed my arms on my hips and pretended to be angry. "Did you ask me if it was okay?"

"Mommy mad," Charlie said to Caleb.

He laughed. "Mommy's not mad. Mommy just needs to sit on a motorcycle too. Let's go find one. Mine isn't here, but there should be a few that belong to your uncles for you to try."

I tried not to cry and walked along beside them. Caleb put his arm around me while carrying Charlie in the other, and just like that, we took our first step as a family.

CHAPTER ELEVEN

Caleb

I had a daughter. Charlie-baby, I heard Amber call her, and that's what she became, my Charlie-baby. I had a million and one fucking regrets about the whole situation. I should have never given up looking for Amber, I'd quit far too fucking soon. More than anything, I should have realized something had happened.

I rolled my shoulder and let out a long, deep breath. I wished Dad could be here to meet his namesake. She had his eyes. They were the same deep brown I also shared with Cane.

Charlie giggled and ran around the yard, chasing Cane who'd stolen her Teddy. He'd make a good dad when his own little one arrived. Something I never would have considered until he met Thea. Maybe I'll be able to step up to the plate the way he has.

I smiled as Amber sidled up beside me and slipped her arm

around my back. "Tom's due to arrive any minute," she said.

"Are you sure you want to go through with this?"

"I should have done it years ago." She made a strange gasping sound, so I turned to look at her.

"It'll be okay. I'll be right there with you."

"I know. It's not that. Just… look at them."

Cane had curled into a ball around the Teddy, and Charlie was climbing all over his back, trying to reach it.

"Uncle Cane," she giggled. "You'll squash him."

He uncurled and fluffed the bear. "Are you saying I'm too big?" he asked and pulled a funny growly face. Charlie squealed and ran in a circle around him, giggling.

"You're both so good with her," Amber said and wiped the tears from her eyes.

"That's cuz she's family."

"Caleb, Amber," Thea called from inside the kitchen.

I turned and saw Tom step into the room behind her. "There's still time to change your mind," I said.

"I'm not going to."

I turned her around and we both went to talk to Tom, while Thea went outside to help Cane with Charlie. Not that he needed any help.

"What's all this about?" Tom asked as we moved our meeting to the living room.

I asked him to take a seat and shut the door. He looked a little nervous and despite the situation, I stifled a smile. A small child hadn't shown me the faintest trace of fear, but Tom looked like he might piss himself if I said boo.

Amber sat on the couch opposite him, and I joined her. "We need to report a crime that happened around four years ago," I said and raised an eyebrow when Tom seemed to sag in relief.

"Four years, that's a very long time ago. What sort of crime are we talking about?"

Amber reached out and grabbed my hand. I squeezed hers in reassurance. "A sexual assault," she said.

When Tom nodded, she proceeded to tell her story.

I listened as the fucking details grew. The story she gave Tom was more in-depth than she'd given me, and I wanted to storm from the house, find the fucker Leo, and pummel him into the ground. I swallowed the anger and rage building inside and told myself that wasn't what Amber wanted. I had to try things her way. I had too much to lose if I didn't.

"Caleb," Amber said and rested her hand on my arm.

"You need a break?"

She smiled. "I'm fine. You're just hurting my hand."

I looked down at my hand clasped in hers and realized I'd been squeezing a bit too hard. I let go and my fingers crunched when I tried to straighten them. I turned my attention to Tom and noticed how white he had gone. Amber's story wasn't pretty by any means, but it couldn't be the first time he's heard or seen worse.

He dropped his head in his hands and looked for a second as though he was about to puke.

"Tom," Amber said, her voice full of concern for him when things should be the other way around.

"I am so fucking sorry," he said and stood to pace the room.

I stood. He backed away, lifted his hand to ward me off, and flicked the safety off his gun holster.

"What the fuck is going on, Tom?" I asked while pulling Amber to stand behind me.

"You gotta understand if I had known any of this I would never…"

My muscles tensed. I wasn't sure if he intended to shoot us or, from the look on his face, himself. "What would you never have done?" I asked, trying to keep my tone soothing.

He paced the room like a caged lion. "You gotta understand. I didn't know. I mean, I knew you and the Feral Sons had some issues, but I thought it was just petty crap, like who gets to go to which bar and shit. When they threw the rock through the window, I knew something was fucking up, I just… I never thought this."

"What did you do?" I asked again.

"I got some gambling debts." His hand hovered over his gun. I pushed Amber tighter into my back. "A lot of fucking gambling debts. I owe Leo Saunders a lot of money. He said that as long as I kept him updated on any place I saw you, he'd give me some space in making the payments."

My nostrils flared. Not caring that he had a fucking gun, I charged across the room and pinned him to the wall. "That's how he knew where to find Amber."

"Yes. I didn't know! I swear!" His pale face became slimy with sweat. He was shit scared, as stupid as hell, and a fucking waste of space as a cop and as a human being. I should have fucking killed him. Instead, I pulled him from the wall before slamming him back into it.

"Does he know where we are now?" I asked.

"No. I swear. I haven't told him anything about you being here. I didn't even know that you were. I just thought I was coming to see Ms. Gerald, and he never mentioned her to me."

"But you mentioned her to him."

He nodded. "I told him I'd seen you visiting an old friend. He asked who, and I told him. I only started to wonder what the hell was going on when the brick was thrown through the window."

"But you could tell him where I am," Amber said, surprising us both with the steel in her voice. "You could call him and say you saw me and Caleb here together."

"I would never—"

"But maybe you should."

Keeping a firm grip on Tom, I turned to face her. "What are you saying?"

She sighed. "If he has one cop reporting to him, how many others are there? How many judges or lawyers? Doing things legally isn't going to work. We have to deal with Leo your way."

"Are you sure?"

"I am. We have our family to protect."

I smiled and released Tom, being certain to take his gun away from him. "Sit," I told him and pointed to the couch.

"Baby, fetch Cane for me, will you?"

Amber left and I sat opposite Tom to keep an eye on him.

"I'm sorry," he said again.

"It's not me you need to apologize to."

We sat in a tense silence for a few minutes before Amber returned with Cane. She must have told him a little of what was going on as he looked ready to rip Tom a new one.

"Leave it," I said. "Tom knows he made a mistake and he's going to help us fix it. Ain't that right?"

Tom gulped but nodded.

"What's the fucking plan?" Cane asked.

Amber answered him. "We're gonna set a trap."

"Here?"

I thought about it for a while but decided this wasn't the best place. We didn't know the area well enough. "Call the guys in," I said. "We'll figure out where and how as soon as they get here."

~

Bono, Jameson, Lucky, and Rex arrived within the hour, as well as a few more of my brothers. They were fucking built like that. If anyone needed anything, they'd be there for them. It had pissed me the fuck off when they'd sided with Cane against me over Thea. At the time, I'd let my hurt and anger regarding Amber cloud my judgment, and thought she was a spoiled fucking princess slumming it with my brother. I couldn't have been more fucking wrong. About both situations. But I should have trusted my blood-brother. The pain I caused him and Thea by telling her stepfather their location would be something I'd regret to my dying day. Maybe that's why I was willing to give Tom a shot at redemption. Sometimes mistakes are too fucking easy to make.

I remembered the day I met each and every one of my brothers. Rex and Lucky, we'd known since childhood. Rex was that geeky kid in school who spent more time on his fucking computer than bothering with anyone around him. He had one hell of a passion for mechanics too.

"Check this fucker out," Cane had said when we'd visited the junkyard looking for an FXDWG seat.

Rex was on the floor surrounded by parts. We watched him in silence as he gathered his pieces together, made notes, and drew up some plans. We came back every fucking day for a week and watched him build a whole, working bike from that scrap. Thirteen years old and he'd done something very few grown-ass men could fucking do. Hell, Cane and I were only a year and two older than him, and we only knew how to build a bike as dad had taught us how from near enough birth. Rex book-taught himself. Said he thought it would take him longer and he wanted to be ready for when he got his learner's permit.

His parents were none too fucking pleased when he started hanging out with Forever Midnight, but Dad soon put their minds at rest. In the end, they decided that at least he was out and not in his room twenty-four-seven. Still, everyone believed he was destined for greater things. Dad even pushed him to go to college, but Rex insisted there was too much to learn and college would only touch the surface of the things he wanted to know. He's a self-taught man, and he has a hell of a lot of respect for it. He and Lucky are the smallest out of the lot of us. They're still packing some fucking muscle but tend towards the leaner side.

Lucky's older than me by a good ten years. His father had been in the club, and I can't remember a time when he wasn't around. After his dad died, he became fucking crazy protective of his Ma. He's fucking awkward as fuck, but he's got the best heart, even if you do have to dig beneath the slimy front he puts on to find it. His real name is Eric, but any fucker who mentions it gets a fist in the face.

That left Jameson and Bono.

I glanced out the window into the backyard. Bono was talking to Cane and Thea. He was a big fucking guy. Not as big as Cane or me, but something in his bearing made him seem larger. Maybe it was the haunted look he carried in his eyes. Who knows what the fuck he saw in the army? He didn't like to talk about it. He'd grown a bit of facial hair in the last few months. Nothing like Cane's. He was far too much of a pretty boy for that.

There were times I envied the relationship he shared with my blood-brother. They were as fucking tight as two peas in a pod. But that was my fucking fault too. After Amber left, I'd blamed her leaving on my decision to stay with Cane and not go away for a break with her. I'd allowed my fucking resentment to put a shadow over our relationship.

Fuck!

There were so many things I'd done wrong. But I'd been working on putting them right.

Jameson leaned into the fridge and pulled out a soda. He had to bend to reach inside. The fucker was six-foot-seven and had to crouch to fit through most doorways. He was the one I knew the least about, but I still trusted him with my fucking life.

He walked into the bar one day about seven years ago. All buttoned up fucking tight in a suit. Walked like he had a fucking stick shoved up his ass, but he was close to breaking and anyone who looked at him knew it. He ditched whatever fucking life he was running from and never looked back. There's a history there that'll come back to bite him on the ass at some point, and when it does, we'll be there for him, just the same as he's always here for us.

Tom sat on a breakfast bar stool, afraid to speak or look at anyone. I moved opposite him.

"You fucking swear to me that you want to make things right with me and with Amber," I said.

"Shit. Of course, I do."

"Then stop looking as though you are about to piss yourself and grow a fucking pair. If Leo spoke to you in the state you're in now, he'd instantly know something was the fuck up."

Amber entered the kitchen and smiled at me. "Charlie's down for a nap," she said.

"In that case, we should figure out what the fuck we're going to do." I called everyone together and filled them in on what had happened. Thea moved toward Amber and held her hand through much of the discussion, and I thanked whatever lucky star had brought her into our lives.

In particular, I related how Tom had been feeding Leo information about my location but stressed that he had come clean on the matter and no one was to hold a fucking grudge. To my amazement, Tom stood ramrod straight under their gazes, giving me a little hope that we could pull off a trap for Leo after all.

"What's the plan?" Lucky said and paced back and forth. "We hiding out and bringing him here?"

"No. Besides the fact that Jameson's friend was good enough to rent us the place at short notice and I'd hate to see it suffer any fucking damage, it's too big, and Leo might suspect an ambush. We need somewhere that Leo would associate with us, but also somewhere he wouldn't expect to find too many brothers hanging out."

Rex cleared his throat and nodded. "Bono's is small. It's secluded, so that minimizes the risk of collateral damage. There's only one road in and out. We know the area and surrounding woodland and could easily watch the property without being seen. Above all, it's small enough to think you wouldn't have much of a guard."

"I'm not sure I'm comfortable with any of you using your own homes," Amber said. "What if things go wrong? He'll know where you live."

"He already knows where I live." Bono looked to Thea. "But it is close to your place."

"He knows where we live too," Cane added.

Thea sighed. "It is a good location," she said, addressing Amber and squeezing her hand before turning to look at Cane as though wanting to say more.

"What is it?" he asked. "Don't worry. Any fucker who tries to come near our home is a dead fucker."

Thea smiled and rubbed her belly, a habit I'd seen her taking up more and more as her baby grew inside her. "It's not that. I just… I just think there are too many things that can go wrong. It could be too easy for him to run into the woods and hide."

"Thea's right," Bono said. "There are too many variables that can go wrong."

"What are our other options?"

No one answered, but Cane walked over to Thea and sat beside her. He whispered something in her ear and when she whispered back, he smiled.

"The floors open to everyone," he said loud enough for us all to hear and making sure to stare each of the brothers down should they dare to suggest otherwise.

"What is it, Thea?" I asked.

"I was just thinking of how it's Sunday and Midnight Anchor closes at 10 pm."

I thought about the bar for a moment. "It's too obvious, Leo would consider the possibility of Amber being there."

As Cane glared at me for not jumping to act on Thea's idea straight away, she continued, "That's why it's perfect. It would be somewhere logical for Amber to be. He would also be able to get someone there before closing to check out how many brothers were on site, and also confirm when they leave. It would be easy to make them think that everyone leaves and just Cherrie, Greg and Amber remain." She turned to Cane and shook her head. "Although now that I say it out loud, I don't think we should put either of them through it."

"I think it has merit," Jameson said.

"I agree," Bono added. "We'd be able to position ourselves remotely and observe the bar, closing in when the time is right."

"I think Greg and Cherrie would want to help." Cane pulled Thea in for a side hug and kissed her head. A wave of nostalgia hit me, and I couldn't help staring at them for a while. They were so incredibly happy together and Cane had become the person he was when we were kids and before Dad died. He was still a broody fucker, but more and more often I saw him smile and heard him laugh. I often wondered if it was Cane who rescued Thea or the other way around.

"Let's go with it," I said. "We just have to work out the details. If it doesn't work and Leo doesn't show, we've lost nothing but time." I didn't add that time might be something we had very little of.

Amber nodded. "I should be there. If this is going to work, then I need to be seen."

"Fuck, no!" Cane said at the same time as I said that it wasn't going to happen.

"We have little choice. If one of Leo's men doesn't see me inside, he'll have no reason to approach."

"I'll do it," Lucky said, causing more than one raised eyebrow. "We're about the same height, even if our build isn't exactly the same. If someone sneaks me in there with a blonde wig, sunglasses, and a blanket covering me, he'll never know the difference."

Rex laughed and shook his head. "You got a blonde wig lying about the house?"

"No, but Ma does. She wore one to a fancy-dress party a few months back."

"I don't know," I said, worried that it might not work.

"Would you prefer to use Amber as bait, or Thea, or Cherrie? There are a hundred and one women we could ask. Hell, I'd bet one of the dolly-girls from the club would do it for a price." When I didn't answer, Lucky sat forward and clenched his fists. "Is that the way you wanna fucking play this?"

I almost growled in frustration, but knew he was right. It was Lucky or no one. Even if I was willing to put some other woman in Amber's place, she sure the fuck wouldn't.

"It's our best bet," Jameson said.

"It'll fucking work too. I didn't get the name Lucky for nothing."

"No, you got that cuz you're lucky every time you find some dolly-girl willing to fuck you," Rex said, smiling.

"Damn right, I fucking am. Every single night."

Rex picked an apple from the countertop and threw it at Lucky's head. Lucky caught it and took a big, sloppy bite. "Lucky scores again," he said through a mouthful.

"We have a location, and bait," I said, nodding to Lucky before placing my hand on Tom's shoulder. "Now all we have to do is figure out when it's best for Tom to trigger it."

The rest of the meeting was spent with more planning. Jameson and Lucky headed out first to call at Lucky's Ma's and collect the wig. Bono followed not far behind them to contact the brothers and let them know something was going down and we'd need their help.

CHAPTER TWELVE

Amber

The plan was simple enough. Thea, Charlie, and I were staying at the safe house with Rex and a couple of brothers keeping watch. Lucky would act as bait while Caleb and around twenty to thirty other brothers hid in the industrial area around the bar to pounce should Leo show up.

They'd been careful to arrive at the safe house separately and were just as careful leaving. Their initial plan was to head to the clubhouse. Then they'd arrange for a large gathering of the brothers to look like they were there while sneaking out to lay in wait.

"Promise me, you'll stay safe," I said to Caleb, as I slipped my arm around his waist.

He and Cane were the last to leave, and while Cane was saying his goodbyes to Thea, we had popped upstairs to check in on Charlie, who was still asleep and blissfully unaware of all the crazy goings-on.

I was reassured by their planning and the fact that Caleb was no longer going after Leo alone, but that didn't mean a well of fear hadn't settled in my stomach like a lead weight.

"I promise, I'll be back before you know it."

I shook my head, pulled the door closed, sealing Charlie away and safe from everything, and fell into his arms. "This feels like we've been planning premeditated murder."

"I've no plan on it coming to that," Caleb said, although he did so just to reassure me. "We'll arm ourselves and approach things with caution. Leo needs to pay for what he's fucking done to you, and for the threats he made. But his Dad and mine were friends once, and I know that the idea of killing him doesn't sit right with you. I'll give him a chance to hand himself in to the police and confess everything. Although, I may have to break every fucking bone in his body before he agrees."

"I just... something doesn't feel right. I have a bad feeling about this."

"I'll be fine." He wrapped his arms tight around me, rested his cheek on the top of my head, and sniffed.

"What are you doing?" I asked.

"Smelling you. You always did smell so fucking good. You know I kept buying your mango scented shampoo even after you left?"

"You did?" I asked, but realized that I'd used it to wash my hair in the shower at his place. "You never used it when we were together."

"I never needed to. I had you to sniff anytime I wanted."

I smiled. "For such a big and hard man on the outside, you have a very squishy center."

"Everyone has a squishy center. That's why we build up the hardness on the outside to keep it safe."

I wasn't quite sure how to respond to that. Throughout the day, I'd managed to talk to both Cane and Thea, and they had said the last twenty-four hours had softened Caleb. Cane said he'd seen him smile for the first time since I left. I was glad that Caleb was becoming the man I knew him to be again, but a part of me wanted him to still have that solid and angry exterior. Maybe that was what he needed to get him through the night and back to me and Charlie. Tears formed in my eyes as I worried about what might be. I hadn't been this scared since he'd left to find his dad's killer, and that had only been one man he was up against and not the entire Feral Sons. They'd talked and talked about it being Leo they were setting a trap for, but everyone knew he wouldn't come alone.

"I'd better go," Caleb said and lifted my chin to kiss me. "I'll make sure Rex keeps you updated."

"You'd better," I said, and we both went downstairs.

Neither Cane nor Caleb had their motorcycles with them, so they jumped in Thea's jeep and pulled away from the house.

Rex stood with us by the front door as we waved goodbye. "Right," he said as soon as they'd driven out of view before showing us an earpiece communication device he was wearing, as well as something that looked a bit like a large battery pack clipped to his belt. "It's not guaranteed to work given the range, but I may be able to keep up-to-date with events in real-time and keep you in the loop. In the meantime, I want you both to stay in the house." He motioned over the two other brothers staying behind. "This is Stan and Billy. Stan will be stationed by the front door and Billy the back. I've been checking out the sweet security system they have here and I'm going to turn it on. If anyone pops a window or opens a door, we'll all know about it instantly."

"Do you think that's likely to happen?" I asked.

"Not really, but Caleb doesn't want us taking any chances. If you hear an alarm, I've checked out the building and found a crawl space at the back of the walk-in closet in the master bedroom. It won't be easy or comfortable," he said looking at Thea. "But that's where I'll need you to go. I'll make my way there too, and ensure you're concealed."

"I think you should leave," I said to Thea.

"I don't. Cane would fucking kill me," Rex said.

"The matter isn't up for debate." Thea grabbed my hand. "Where you stay, I stay. You know the brothers. They're just being overly cautious anyway. Nothing's going to happen."

That well of dread in my belly turned into a fucking boulder. I wished I had Thea's faith that everything would be fine, but nothing had ever worked out the way I wanted it to. Why would tonight be any different?

My heart beat way too fast as I followed her through the house. Thea was lovely and it was great that she'd defeated her demons, but mine were still out there.

"How do you cope?" I asked as we moved into the kitchen. The place had fast become the epicenter of the house. A place where we could gather and keep busy.

"What do you mean?" she replied while taking one of the barstools.

Her eyes drifted toward the back door. I followed her gaze and noted Billy stationed outside. He'd pulled one of the garden chairs next to the door and sat on it with his head leaned back against the wall. Some sentry he'd make if he fell asleep.

"Sophia told me what your stepbrother did to you. I think she wanted to reassure me that things would get better. That you were okay, and I would be too." My breath hitched, uncertain if I should continue or if dredging up the past would be too painful for Thea. "Did he... did he really torture you?"

Thea reached out and grabbed my hand. I'd noted over the last few days that she was more tactile than most people are with strangers. It surprised me, but also had a strange way of making me feel as though I could open up to her.

"Daniel was not a nice person," she said after a moment. "I feared and hated him in equal measure for years. There are some nights I still have nightmares, some nights where I hear a noise downstairs and worry for the briefest of seconds that it might be him. Then I remember, he's gone. The only power he has is to instill a remembered fear. He had so much power over me in life, I'm determined that he will have very little over me in death. It's not a matter of coping, it's a matter of allowing myself to live free from his influence."

"Sophia mentioned that he died. Maybe it's easier to move on because you know he can't come back."

She smiled. "Maybe. Or maybe it's because Cane killed him, and I know he'd do the same to anyone else who ever tried to hurt me or our baby."

I tilted my head and looked at her. She really was stunning. With thick brown hair and large green eyes. Even with her tall stature and pregnancy belly, she seemed almost fragile. But there was a steely glint in her eyes that made her look older than her years.

"Sophia never told me that Cane killed him," I said.

"She didn't know. It's not exactly something I spread around."

"I guess not." I sighed and looked out the window. Dull, gray clouds filled the sky and it looked like it might rain. "Caleb said he'll give Leo a chance to turn himself in. Do you think he will?"

"Do I think Caleb will give him a chance or do I think Leo will turn himself in?"

"Either. Both."

"Caleb will do whatever you want him to. As for Leo, I've never met him, but from the little I know, I doubt he would willingly go to the police and confess anything."

"I don't know. Caleb can be quite persuasive when he wants."

Thea raised an eyebrow and laughed. "I'm sure he can be."

I laughed back. At that moment, my phone rang.

"Hi Sophia," I said, having seen her name on the display before I answered.

"Hey, chica. Just wanted to see how you're doing."

"I'm great. I'm actually here with Thea." I glanced at her and smiled. She asked me to give Sophia her love, which I did.

"I take it everything is still A-Okay with Caleb and Charlie."

"Better than I could have ever imagined. You were right, I should have come clean years ago."

"Ah, well. I don't like to toot my own horn, but I am known to be right on occasion."

I laughed. "Don't let it go to your head."

"Me? Never. I take it this means you have a plus one to my wedding. That's if you think it'll all be over by then."

"It'll be over. Caleb and his brothers are out right now seeing to it."

"That is a relief," she said, and it was clear she was telling the truth from the tone in her voice. "Mom and Pop are making friendly with these bikers watching our every move like hawks, but Ben's starting to feel like a caged bird."

I sighed. "I am sorry about that," I said.

"He'll get over it."

"Tell him it will be all over soon."

The kitchen door opened, and Rex came in carrying Charlie. "Look who I found up and around," he said.

"I gotta go, Sophia. I'll call you tomorrow. Hopefully, your bodyguards will be gone by then." With that, I ended the call, stood, and reached my arms out to hold my sweet baby girl. "Good afternoon, Charlie-baby. Did you have a nice nap?"

"Play outside," she said. "Uncle Rex motorcycle."

My skin tingled at her words and a strange lightness came over me. Charlie had gone from having only me, Sophia, Caroline, and Franc in her social circle to now having Uncles coming at her from all corners.

"It's going to rain," I said. "We have to stay indoors. Shall we go and find something to watch on cable?"

"Peppa," she said and wriggled in my arms to go down. "Aunt Thea, Peppa."

Thea giggled as Charlie pulled her from the stool and dragged her from the room. "What's Peppa," she mouthed back at me.

I rolled my eyes. She'd find out soon enough and have to watch it five times a day for anywhere up to the next six years.

CHAPTER THIRTEEN

Caleb

After leaving the safe house, Cane and I headed straight to the clubhouse. He drove as it was Thea's car, but my skin prickled. "Could you go any fucking slower?" I asked.

He smirked and glared at me out of the corner of his eye. "As a matter of fact, I *fucking* can. Would you like me to?"

"Go fuck yourself."

Cane laughed but didn't change the speed he was driving. I turned my attention out the window, knowing that keeping to the speed limit was probably the best course of action. Clouds drifted together, blanketing the sky. That's all we needed: rain.

"Looks like we're gonna get wet." Cane gave me a double-take before noting where I was looking. He laughed again and shook his head. Fucking juvenile.

I decided to ignore him and switched on the comms unit Rex

had given me. The crazy fucker carried a set of five in the trunk of his car and had dished them out to each of us before we left. Only Lucky had to go without, but he was with Jameson and could stay in touch through him if necessary.

"Switch your comms unit on," I said to Cane.

He shifted in his seat and did so. Rex said he'd tested them, and they were all working, but it wouldn't hurt for me to check and be sure.

"Can you hear me?" I asked Cane. Before he had the chance to come back with some smart comment, I added, "through the fucking earpiece."

He grinned as though reading my mind but confirmed he could. I nodded, and we switched them off again. Rex had advised us all to turn them on at 7 pm to conserve battery power.

By the time we pulled up at the clubhouse, around twenty other brothers were already there. These were the members of Forever Midnight who would stay here and make it look like I was too. Both mine and Cane's bikes were among those parked outside.

A wave of dread roiled my stomach when I stepped from the car and the first droplet of rain landed on my face. We made a show of standing and chatting with a couple of brothers outside for a while, just in case Leo had some other fucker on his payroll watching me.

Inside, we moved through the crowd of brothers. Their heads turned in our direction, each ready and waiting to help where needed. I deliberately asked those with family or loved ones to stay here. And Bono had arranged for volunteers out of the rest. A few had been asked to go to Midnight Anchor and hang out. Greg and Cherrie would serve them alcohol-free beer, but they were to make it look like they were drinking. Others had been given strict instructions to stay away from the place as well as timeslots for pickup and transportation. We didn't want a truckload of Forever Midnight at the bar or on the road headed in that direction.

After a few conversations and the swift decline of more offers of help, I took a deep breath and grabbed Cane, who'd met up with Bono among the crowd, and the three of us went to my office.

"Everything set?" I asked.

Bono nodded. "Jameson just called. He and Lucky made their way into the bar and to the spare room upstairs. They are going to make it look like a woman and guard are in the room through the curtains." He moved to the window ledge and perched on its edge.

Despite the burst of sheet rain that now fell from the sky and rattled the window, the day was still warm, and the air conditioning system blasted waves of cool air around the room.

I wasn't looking forward to hunkering down in the rain and laying in wait, but I wanted this over and done with. We all did.

I sighed, opened the drawer on my desk, and pulled out the key to the gun cabinet fastened to the wall. I fucking hated using guns. It wasn't our style. But we couldn't expect the Feral Sons to operate by the same standards we did and would need them for back-up.

"I'll take the SIG," Bono said, opting for his old service weapon.

"That leaves the Glock for you and the Ruger for me," I said to Cane while handing out the guns as well as some flashlights.

"Let's get this fucking over with," said Cane.

I nodded, and we slipped down the back steps. We avoided the crowds, but the deep rumble of their voices vibrated through the walls. We slipped all the way down to the basement level where a concealed hatch led to a small tunnel. We hadn't used the thing in years. It came in fucking handy for my Dad and the other club members back in the day though. Back when the activities of Forever Midnight were not always on the up and up. Cobwebs and a dankness clogged the air, and dust particles flickered in the light from our flashlights. We had to crouch, and our shoulders brushed up against the walls as the tunnel wasn't built for men the size of us.

"Fuck," Cane said as a spattering of debris, caused by the

activity of people and vehicles above, dislodged from the ceiling and landed on his head.

I stifled a laugh. He was never any fucking good in tight spaces. That's why he loved living in the mountains so much.

He attempted to stand upright and banged his head, cussed, and dropped his flashlight in the process.

Bono turned back and shone the light of his own flashlight in his face.

"You done?" he asked when Cane finally stopped cussing. "Or are you gonna carry on until every fucker in a hundred miles hears you and comes to check out what the hell's going on?"

Cane only growled at him in response. There weren't many people who could get away with talking to him like that. Bono was lucky he counted among their number.

After about ten minutes, we emerged into the pouring rain a fair distance away from the clubhouse.

"What took you so long?" Cherrie said as she stuck her crazy pink-haired head out the window of Greg's pick-up and flashed us a devilish grin. "Damn near thought I'd turn to a dried-out old husk before you boys showed up."

"Cane thought it would be fun to have a hissy fit in the tunnel," I said while jabbing him with my elbow.

"I'll give you a fucking hissy fit," he said while Bono smiled.

I chuffed, and shook my head, rushing to jump in the pickup before Cane decided he was fucking in charge and stole the front seat. Seconds after I'd closed the door, Bono and Cane hopped in the back seats.

"Tom doing okay with Greg?" I asked Cherrie.

"You bet he is."

Greg had been pretty fucked up by Thea's stepbrother, and it had slowed him down. He was in his late sixties now and not as quick to heal as he once was. But he was still one hell of a fucker to be reckoned with and would make sure Tom played his part the way he was meant to.

I leaned back in the car seat and enjoyed the calm before the storm. We were thirty minutes out from our meeting spot, where Cherrie would drop us to meet the other brothers.

Throughout the ride my emotions churned, and images flashed in my mind like fucking pulsating lights set to drive me insane. My head pounded along with the rain, and the incessant swish of the wipers set my nerves on edge. Despite the worry that hardened my gut for Amber and Charlie, it felt good to be out with a clear purpose with my brothers. Too often, I spent my time checking over business records or dealing with petty fucking disputes. Tonight, we moved as one with a clear purpose, something we hadn't done since rescuing Thea from her family. We were out to get Leo. We had direction. All we had to hope was that the fucker showed his face.

I gave a wry chuckle. I may look like I'd driven my bike into a tank as Lucky put it, but I'd landed a fair few punches on Leo's mug before he'd turned tail and ran, so I was betting he wasn't exactly a fucking pretty picture himself.

"You all think this is gonna work?" Cherrie said after a moment.

"It'll work," I said. "As soon as I give the word, Tom's set to call Leo and tell him he saw me at the clubhouse—"

"And how's that gonna work exactly when you want him to go to the bar?"

I smiled. Cherrie had a heart of gold, but she had the patience of a black mamba and could be just as aggressive when confronted. "He's also gonna tell him that my friend Amber Gerald was staying out at the bar and that I'd asked him to call in to see her. When he got there, she was resting, so he's going back in the morning."

My stomach rolled. It wasn't much of a plan, but we couldn't be sure that anyone had seen the disguised Lucky arrive, but they would see Tom. A cop tends to stick out, and his having been there would add weight to the story.

"You're thinking Leo's gonna show up to stop Amber from talking," Cherrie said as she signaled off the main road and turned into a parking lot a block away from the bar.

"That's the plan." Not much of one, I admitted to myself

again, but I thought Leo would buy it. He was never the smartest fucker in any room.

CHAPTER FOURTEEN

Caleb

"Fuck. I'm fucking going insane. This is driving me fucking insane."

It was 9:30 and there was no sign of Leo or any other fucker from the Feral Sons.

I banged my fist on the wall where I crouched under the cover of the parking lot, hiding from view on the third story with Cane and ten other brothers. Bono had left us to take up another vantage point with the same number again. The bar pulsed with fucking music that set my teeth on edge. Around eight Forever Midnight club members were inside, and another two milled about under what little cover there was in the bar's lot. Normally, you'd see more people hanging about, but even though the rain had eased a little, it had driven everyone inside.

I cursed my fucking luck and wished that we'd given Greg

Cane's comms unit. Then I'd know what the fuck was going on, but there was no way he could have used it without being seen anyway.

"Report, Cane." Bono's voice sounded in my earpiece. "You seen any movement yet?"

"Nothing yet," Cane reported.

Fucking right there was nothing yet. I would have at least expected one fucker to be checking the place out. Tom had made the call as planned over an hour ago. It shouldn't have taken that long for Leo to mobilize his men.

"Rex," I said, fearing the worst. "You still with us?"

"I'm here," he said, but his voice was overlaid with static. "But the weather is causing some interruption."

"Everything good your end?"

"All good and locked up tight."

I nodded even though I knew he couldn't see me. I wanted to ask him to put Amber on the comms, but an irrational fear that if I did, our cover would be blown made my heart burn. Instead, I never took my eyes off the bar.

After a while, people started to emerge. They milled about by the door, their minds muddled by alcohol, drugs, or both. Not a single fucker seemed likely to report to Leo. Most could barely stand up straight. Slowly they moved away. Some jumped in cabs when they arrived. Others banded together with designated drivers, driving away with music blaring from their speakers to rival that still coming from the bar. Their cars rumbled to life and tires squealed as they pulled away.

Greg usually ran a tight ship and never let any fucker leave in their car if they'd had too much to drink, but I guess our minds were all on something else tonight.

My brothers were the last to leave, but still, we watched, and we waited. A light came on in an upstairs window and I noted the silhouette of the top of a head that looked like it had long hair. I had to admit, if I didn't know it was Lucky, I'd be fooled into thinking it was a woman, but I wasn't sure I'd be convinced it was Amber.

"The bar's empty." Jameson's voice sounded in my earpiece. That meant only he, Lucky, Greg, and Cherrie remained inside.

A rumble followed his message, and a burst of rain followed suit as the heavens opened.

"Fuck," Cane said. "I can barely see two feet in front of my face through this fucking shit." The overcast sky had darkened further with nightfall. That, along with the rain, made it almost impossible to see anything.

"Bono. You still got eyes on the door?" I asked.

"Negative. Visibility's reduced."

I sighed and huffed out a breath. "We're gonna have to change positions. Stay low and move in small groups, keeping an eye on the building when you can."

The sky rumbled again and the hairs on the back of my neck bristled as the rain and wind picked up. If Leo had two fucking brain cells to rub together, he wouldn't come out in this shit. He had until morning for the weather to change, and as far as he knew, Amber wasn't going anywhere.

I was about to curse my fucking luck and settle in for the long haul when Cane nudged me and nodded along the road. "We've got company," he said.

A spattering of light flickered through the rain and I realized the rumble I'd heard wasn't thunder. It came from bikes. From the headlights, I counted six motorcycles, but it was fucking impossible to see if Leo was amongst their riders.

Hot burning anger built inside me as they drove straight up to the bar and stopped their engines. They hesitated for a moment and through the haze it looked as though one of them was on the phone. From the shape and size of him it could have been Leo, but I couldn't be a hundred percent fucking certain. My main concern at that moment in time was that someone had rumbled our plan and was letting him know. But the phone soon went away, and the fuckers dismounted.

"We're on the move," I said. "As soon as they're all inside. We block the exits and enter."

I steeled myself. The muscles throughout my body strained

and tightened. As I'd told Amber, I may not be planning to kill Leo — I had every intention of offering him the chance to turn himself in — but I sure as fuck was expecting to.

I turned to look at Cane and he nodded. His determination reflected my own. We raced down the stairwell. Although it provided some cover, it was open to the elements, and puddles of rainwater mingled with others of piss. The fucking place stank. We ignored the stench and sped down the concrete steps before halting at the door below. I opened it ajar and poked my head out. The rain had eased in the brief moments of our journey, and I was able to note that we'd arrived just in time to see the bar door closing behind the last fucker. They'd gone straight in the main entrance. And seeing as I knew there was no fucking way Greg hadn't locked it. They had to have broken the lock.

"They're inside," I said through the comms to Bono.

"On our way," he answered. "Where are you?"

"We're leaving the lot now."

"Don't be seen," he answered as though it was my intention to fucking fire off a ticker-tape parade to announce our arrival.

After one final check to make sure the coast was clear, we slipped into the street, being sure to keep to the shadows.

"Any action your end, Jameson?" Cane asked.

"Nothing yet. But I can hear movement in the bar."

"Be ready," I said.

"We're in position," Bono said as I hopped on the pavement and motioned to Cane to take up position on the other side of the door. The lock was busted open, and it gaped a little, but not enough to see inside. Given the time they'd had, the Feral Son' had to be beyond the small greeting area that led into the main bar area by now.

As Cane and I drew our weapons, our other brothers separated into two groups behind us and followed suit. After Cane nodded to signify he was ready, I let Bono and Jameson know we were going inside.

Cane nudged the door open with his foot. We entered the bar, covering each other's backs. The light overhead bathed the confined space in light.

"We're in," I whispered into my mouthpiece before asking two brothers to stay behind to cover the door.

I stayed restrained, waiting for Bono and Jameson to respond before charging forward. Even though adrenaline pumped through my body at the fucking speed of light, my heartbeat thundered in my ears, and I wanted nothing more than to charge headlong into the bar and take Leo out, I had to keep my head for Amber's sake. Instead, I quietly edged toward the main door, leading to the bar and waited for Jameson and Bono to report they were ready to move in.

When Jameson said he had them in his sight and that Leo

was among them, I gave the order to close in and swung the second door open.

As soon as I did, all fucking hell broke loose.

CHAPTER FIFTEEN

Caleb

Leo and his men didn't know which way to turn, but without hesitation, they opened fire. Cane rolled and flipped a table. A bullet impacted the wood above his head, causing it to splinter. I scrambled into the room, taking cover behind another table. More bullets hit the mirror and bottles lining the wall behind the bar. The room filled with the sound of breaking glass and the sweet, sickly scent of liquor.

I peeked around the edge of my table. Leo and his fuckers were nowhere in sight. But the trajectory of their bullets told me they were close to the restrooms. As the thought popped in my mind, I worried that they'd be able to make it out the small windows inside, but I knew that was impossible. They were too high to gain easy access to and too small to squeeze through.

Everything became still, and the only sound was my

breathing.

"Come out and fight me like a fucking man," I called into the too-quiet room.

Leo laughed. "You'd fucking like that, wouldn't you?"

"Yeah. I fucking would, you pussy."

"Always trying to prove how much better you are than me." I looked at Cane, and he shrugged. Neither of us had a clue what the fucker was talking about.

"Caleb doesn't need to prove fucking shit," Cane said. "He's always been better than you."

Leo laughed again, but this time there was a bitter tone to it. "Yeah, so my Pa told me," he snarled.

I looked at the floor and stared at the ugly blue diamond pattern on the carpet until it made my head hurt.

"Is that what all this is fucking about," I said. "Trying to prove something to your dead fucking Pa? All this trouble has been over some fucking petty insecurity issues you have about not being good enough."

"FUCK YOU, FUCK MY PA, AND FUCK NOT BEING GOOD ENOUGH."

His voice sounded more and more agitated, and footsteps echoed around the room. I leaned around the edge of the table to try and get a better view.

A shot rang out.

A bullet grazed my arm but missed any substantial target.

"I AM FUCKING BETTER THAN YOU. I fucked your girl to prove that. Thought that would fuck you up. But her leaving did that better than I ever could." Leo laughed, and I realized just how crazy and unhinged he really was. "It's been pitiful to see how far you've fallen in the last few years. If Pa had lived to see the man you became, he'd see how pathetic you've always been."

My mind fucking whirled. Years of problems over some petty jealousy. When I thought of what he did to Amber, I wanted to pound his fucking face. The crazy thing was, in his fucked-up mind, he thought that made him a better man than me. His definition of a man and mine were way fucking different.

I growled, and my muscles tightened. It was time to end this.

Before I had the chance to say anything, Cane shouted out to the other Feral Sons. "Your president is fucking crazy. Any fucking idiot can see that. This isn't going to end well. For you, or for him. I'm gonna give you one fucking chance to lay your guns down and get the fuck out of here. If Leo wants to prove how much better he is than Caleb, he can fucking fight him one on one."

"Or he can turn himself in and go to fucking prison for what he did to Amber," I added, although I hoped that wasn't the option he would take.

A murmur of voices followed suit. Then, one after the other, five guns were thrown into the center of the room.

"Fuck you, you fuckers," Leo said with a note of panic in his voice.

He walked into full view. His gun was held in the air above his head. I stood and faced him, while my brothers came out of their hiding places with every one of their guns trained on him.

He glanced over his shoulder at his men who emerged behind him, their hands raised in the air above their heads.

Cane motioned them to the exit we'd come through. "See them out and secure them," he said to our brothers nearest the door.

"Good fucking riddance," Leo called at their backs.

He dropped his gun to the floor, and my brothers lowered theirs. I placed mine on the ground by my feet.

"You made a decision?" I asked.

Leo casually walked over to the nearest chair, smashed it on the floor, and removed a leg from the broken pieces.

"I guess you have," I said as he hefted it in his hand.

Heart thumping, I barreled forward, driving into Leo like a battering ram. He flew backward, managing to keep his footing. He smashed the chair leg into my arm. The fucker aimed a second swing at my head.

I ducked. Anger swept through my veins. Years and years of

suffering all cuz this fucker had Daddy issues. I lashed out with a sweeping kick to his leg. And missed. But didn't let up.

He swung the leg at me again. This time, I caught it, twisting it in his hands. He had two choices: let it go or risk breaking his fucking wrist by keeping ahold of it. He let go.

I dropped it, punched him in the face, and smashed my foot into the back of his leg. His knee buckled, sending him to the ground. He flailed around for the chair leg. I kicked it out of his way and punched him again, holding onto his collar to stop him from falling.

He laughed.

I stopped.

Blood dripped from his nose. His lip was cut in a second place, and his eye was black from our earlier encounter. Still, he sat on the ground laughing at me.

"You think you've won," he said and spat a clump of blood at my feet. "But my men are with the girl and know what to do with her."

His words were like a stab wound to the fucking chest. "Rex," I called into my comms unit. "Rex, fucking answer me."

I turned to Cane and saw my own panic mirrored in his eyes. They darted from me and back to Leo on the floor behind me. Before I had a chance to turn, a gunshot rang out.

In the blink of an eye, Leo had pulled a second gun. But

somebody shot him before he had the chance to shoot me. I looked back at Cane. In the doorway behind him, the one we sent Leo's men out, Tom emerged, gun in hand.

He put it away and walked toward me, looking down at Leo. "I heard there was a break-in," he said. "I'll call it in and let them know I've got the perp."

A strange gurgling noise came from Leo. I looked at his face. Blood bubbled from his mouth and dripped down the lion tattoo on his neck. It took me a while to realize he was still laughing.

"She... she'll be dead by morning," he said. His final words.

"Rex," I called again. There was still no answer.

CHAPTER SIXTEEN

Amber

"Are you okay?" Thea asked.

I looked at the untouched bagel on the plate in my hands, placed them both on the end table, and stared at the clock on the wall. It was a little after ten. Rex had been in a few minutes ago to let us know that Caleb, Cane, and the others were still watching the bar and that there was nothing to report yet. Although, he was concerned that the weather was playing havoc with his comms signal, as he called it, and he was worried he would lose contact with the others.

"I can't stand sitting here, waiting, not knowing what's going on or if he's safe. How can you be so calm?"

Thea sighed. "Maybe I'm just good at not showing how worried I am."

"I'm sorry."

"It's fine. I am trying to be calm, for the sake of the baby, but it's not as easy as you may think. I guess I'm just good at hiding away my true feelings."

I gave her a wry smile. "I'm pretty good at that myself."

Thea took a sip of water and glanced at Charlie. She was curled asleep on the couch next to me. I hadn't wanted to put her back to bed when she fell asleep. I was too worried that something might happen, and I wouldn't be able to reach her.

"It must have been hard staying away from Caleb when you obviously never stopped loving him."

"Some days it was easier than others." The sound of the rain, battering the windows, and the wind outside made my head pound. I wished for all the world that the weather would change, and Rex could listen in to what was happening back in Castle Rock.

"I knew he would be upset and hurt," I continued, talking about Caleb. "I guess... I just told myself that he would soon move on and get over me. I thought it was for the best. I wanted to stop him—" I huffed and shook my head "—I wanted to stop a night like this from happening."

"Soon it will be over, and we can go back to worrying about making Sophia's wedding day the best she's ever had."

"I just wish I could be there for her now. We were meant to be spending some time together before the big day, and now she's had to do everything by herself."

"She understands."

"I know. That's what makes it so much worse."

The wind rose and lashed the rain against the window. "Let's watch a show and drown out the noise. It'll give us something to focus on." Thea lifted the controller and glanced at Charlie again. "Sorry," she said. "I didn't think. Will the noise wake her?"

I smiled. "If the storm hasn't woken her, I doubt any noise from the television will. She's a pretty heavy sleeper."

Thea smiled and turned on the television, flicking through channels until we settled on something to watch. But the windows rattled, and the house moaned, and it became harder and harder to focus on anything else.

"It's a good job Rex brought Billy and Stan inside or they'd be on the brink of hypothermia by now," Thea said after a while.

I stood and moved the curtains to look outside. It was pitch black with nothing to be seen except the occasional shadows of branches moving in the wind. "These old houses are lovely, but in weather like this, you do get the sense of being battered about like a ship at sea."

Thea joined me at the window. "At least we don't have the chance of sinking."

Before I could respond, the lights dimmed, and the television shut off. For a few heartbeats, the lights flickered as though fighting to stay on. But they too shut off, plunging the room into complete darkness.

Thea grabbed out for my hand.

"Charlie," I said, and we moved in unison to the couch, feeling our way in the dark.

I lifted Charlie in my arms but pushed my foot against Thea's to make sure we kept in contact. I strained through the bustle of the storm, listening for any sound that was out of the ordinary. There was none.

"I can't hear Rex or the others moving around," Thea said, and I realized she was right. "I think we should go to the hiding place Rex mentioned."

I don't know how long I stood there, too afraid to move or even breathe. I was convinced that if I listened long and hard enough, I'd hear Rex and the others calling out our names. He knew where we were.

"Okay," I whispered eventually and pulled Charlie tighter against me.

Thea reached for my hand and I felt how cold and clammy it had become.

"We'll be fine," I said, although from the nausea churning in my stomach I wasn't sure we would be. "The storm probably put the power out."

"I know. I'm just… I'm not very good in the dark."

I held her hand tighter. Neither was I.

"I can feel the couch against my leg, so that means the door is this way." Thea tugged me to the right, and I followed.

We groped along the wall until we found the door. I was breathing fast, and my heartbeat thundered when we opened it. Beyond, the hallway lay in complete darkness.

We froze. My breath hitched, and I sensed that Thea's had too. "I don't think we'll be able to find the hiding spot in the dark," I said.

"Let's go to the kitchen. I saw a box of matches in one of the drawers. We can use them."

"There might be a flashlight or some candles in there too." I pulled Thea in the direction of the kitchen, feeling along the walls as I went.

"I can just about make out the shape of things," Thea said. "I think my eyes are adjusting to the light."

"In that case, we'll be faster if you lead. I still can't see a thing."

We did move faster as Thea's steps became more confident. Within seconds, we were in the kitchen. With the large windows and open curtains, I was also able to discern my surroundings in the dim light.

"Over here," Thea said and raced to a drawer by the cooker.

Footsteps sounded in the hallway. I dashed after her. The

wind continued its incessant howl and the rain bashed the house as though determined to wash it from the face of the Earth. I reached up and grabbed a pan from the rack over the center island to use as a weapon if necessary, and Thea and I crouched behind the kitchen unit. I hugged Charlie's warm body close to my own and for the first time in a very long time, prayed.

The footsteps moved through the house. There was a thud followed by a cuss. The person moved closer.

"Thea," a voice I recognized called. "Amber."

A breath of air rushed from my body. Tears of relief welled in my eyes.

Thea stood. "Billy," she said at the same time as a dark figure pushed through the door.

"Thank fuck," he answered. "Cane would have ripped my fucking head off."

"What's happening?" Thea asked as I found my feet.

"Rex was worried about a power outage and said he'd seen a generator out back while searching the grounds. He and Stan went to see if it was in working order."

"Where were you?" I asked unable to keep the note of accusation from my voice.

I couldn't see Billy's face clearly, but from his stance, I sensed he was embarrassed by the answer. "I was upstairs using the little boys' room," he answered after a moment.

I laughed. The whole situation was so ridiculous, it was the only thing to do.

Before I had the chance to compose myself the lights flickered on and stayed that way. A minute or so later, Rex and Stan joined us in the kitchen.

"Generator's working," Rex said, and I laughed again.

Thea smiled at me and asked if the comms unit was working.

Rex shook his head. "Cell signal is flashing in and out though."

For the next ten minutes, we all stayed together in the kitchen. Neither Thea nor I were too keen to be on our own again.

Billy had made Charlie a makeshift bed on the kitchen counter and I sat at one of the stools with my hand on her to stop her from rolling off while she slept. I only moved when my cell beeped and vibrated on the countertop where I'd left it earlier in the day. I rushed to check, hoping it was a message Caleb managed to get through.

I almost dropped the phone when I read it.

"What's wrong?" Thea was by my side in seconds.

"It's from Sophia. She's hiding. There's someone in her house."

"Fuck," Rex said. "We gotta reach Caleb."

CHAPTER SEVENTEEN

Caleb

Cane and I rushed to Greg's pickup with the intention of heading back to the safe house. My stomach rolled and from the cording in Cane's neck, he was fit to kill every fucker in sight if anything had happened to Thea.

A part of me thought that Leo's final words were one last fuck over of my mind, one final way he could beat me at something, but a nagging voice in my head kept reminding me of the phone call I'd seen his group take before they entered the bar.

"Fuck," I said and banged my fists on the roof of the pickup.

"Save it for when you need it," Cane said, so I huffed out a breath and tried to calm the fuck down.

I reached for the door when a crackle sounded in my ears. "Caleb, Cane, Bono. Any fucker hear me?"

Cane and I froze. "Rex. Thank fuck. I can barely read you. Is everyone safe?"

"Amber, Thea, and Charlie are all fine." I flung my head back and clenched my head in relief.

"Who's in trouble?" Cane asked, always more perceptive than me.

My relief was short-lived. My throat dried and I found it hard to swallow when he told us Amber had received a message from Sophia a few minutes ago. She was back home, hiding, and someone was in her house.

"Fuck," Cane said, echoing my earlier words.

We jumped in the pickup and raced towards the bungalow. Cane threw his phone at me. "Sophia's number is saved on there. Thea gave it to me when you went to Ta-Towhee."

I scrolled through the phone and searched, while he sped off. This time, I didn't comment on his speed. I doubted the truck could go any fucking faster.

When I estimated we were five minutes away, I dialed Sophia's number, prayed she had the sense to turn the ringer off, and waited.

"Hello," she whispered, and I resisted growling in relief.

"It's Caleb. Don't speak, don't make a sound. Turn the volume way down and listen. If I say anything that isn't true, I want you to press something on the screen. You won't hear anything, but I will," I said, and decided to start with the obvious. "There's someone in your house and you're hiding."

No beep.

"There's one man."

Beep.

"Two."

Beep.

"Three." No beep. "Good girl, you're doing fine. Cane and I are almost with you."

"Three," Cane mouthed, and I nodded.

"It'll help us to know where you're hiding," I continued. I didn't add that was in case this turned into a shoot-out, and I didn't want her in the fucking firing line. "You're under a bed." Beep. "In a wardrobe." Beep. I had to think for a while. My fucking brain hurt with the effort. "The bathtub." Beep.

I covered the phone and turned to Cane. "Where the fuck do people hide?" I asked.

He shrugged, but then it looked as though a lightbulb went off inside his head. "Thea once mentioned that she used to hide under the sink in the kitchen when she was little."

I thought it was a fucking long shot but asked if she was there.

No beep.

Cane pulled the car to a stop a way down the street from

the bungalow, we could just see it. A light was on, and a shadow moved past the broken window.

"We're outside," I said. "I'm ending the call—"

Beep.

"I have to, to come in. Hang tight, we'll be with you in a second." Without waiting for another answer, I hung up.

Cane gave me a tight look and we got out of the pickup.

We jogged across the road, staying low and to the shadows. When we reached the building, we pressed tight against the wall. "How do you want to play this?" I asked.

"Same way I like to play everything," he answered. "By walking straight up to the fucking door."

Despite the fucking situation, I smiled and clapped him on the shoulder. "Straight up to the fucking door it is."

I stood tall and, next to my blood-brother, walked up to the door and knocked. "We know you're in there," I said. "You should know, Leo's dead, and if you fuckers don't come out with your hands in the air, you'll find yourselves in the same fucking predicament."

A shuffle sounded and, after a while, someone said, "I'm coming out."

The door opened. One fucker walked out with his hands on his head. He moved slowly, edging in a circle around us as though trying to get us to turn. Cane smirked, grabbed hold of the door and yanked it backward into the house. The crack and cry of pain as it impacted a second fucker rang through the neighborhood. A dog barked.

I punched the fucker who thought he could fool us in the face. Seeing we meant business, the final fucker put his hands up and surrendered for real.

"Is Leo really dead?" he asked.

"He is," I answered.

"Thank fuck for that," he said with evident relief on his face. The others stood and echoed the sentiment.

I left Cane to deal with them, went to the kitchen, and opened the cupboard under the sink. Sure enough, crammed inside I found Sophia.

"You're gonna be okay," I said. "It's over."

CHAPTER EIGHTEEN

Amber

It seemed an eternity that I sat in the living room waiting for Caleb to return to the safe house. The storm had subsided, and full cell coverage returned.

Thea and I had spent an age on the phone with Sophia, and we were happy to note that she seemed her normal chirpy self after her ordeal. Cane and Caleb were dropping her back at Ben's before making their way here. No doubt the two who were set to guard her were about to receive an earful.

Charlie had remained asleep and blissfully unaware, and after the call, I decided that she could finally be settled in bed. Tomorrow would bring another exciting day, and the day after was Sophia's wedding.

My heart felt like it would leap from my chest when a pickup pulled up outside. Thea beat me to the door, running outside and flinging herself into Cane's arms. He wasted no time in sweeping her inside, and I thanked my lucky stars that their room was the furthest away from Charlie's.

Caleb stood by the vehicle, staring at me for a while, and my old worries surfaced. He'd changed his mind; he didn't want me or Charlie. Who could blame him with all the trouble I'd caused?

I swallowed down the lump forming in my throat. "What's wrong?" I asked, deciding it best to broach the subject.

"Nothing. You're just so fucking perfect, and with the hall light glowing behind you, you look like an angel. I just wanted to look at you for a while."

"You did?"

"I do."

"Well, you know, I'm not going anywhere, so you're gonna have to look at me forever."

"Sounds like heaven," he said as he walked to the doorway to meet me.

Fire exploded in my veins as Caleb pulled me close and sealed my lips in a kiss hot enough to start a forest fire. He growled and gathered his arms around me, lifted me, and carried me up the stairs. He kicked open the door, and my fingers instantly went to my mouth to shush him.

"We can't wake Charlie," I said, and Caleb caught the door at the last moment, stopping it from banging.

Being more careful, he closed it tight, and then whirled me around and pressed my back firmly against the wall. I moaned as he trailed his lips along my neck and gently sucked on my ear. His fingers tangled in my hair. I lost myself in the sensation and the whirlwind of emotions that flared within me.

I bit his bottom lip. He growled again.

I lifted my T-shirt over my head and removed my bra as Caleb tugged my jeans and panties from my lower body.

My heart thundered. I needed Caleb. I'd always needed Caleb. I'd just been too stupid, too afraid, and too broken to realize it.

He stripped from his clothes and flipped me around. His hand snaked around my waist and drew my back tight against him. My whole fucking body responded to his touch. Heat pooled in my core as I felt the bulge of his cock, straining against my bottom.

With one arm wrapped around my stomach, the other entwined in my hair and pulled my head back. Caleb held me in place and nuzzled the side of my neck, while his other hand traveled over my body and up to my breast. My nipples hardened as Caleb teased one between his fingers, tweaking and pinching until I couldn't take any more.

I leaned into him, rested my head on his shoulder, and twisted it so my lips could reach his own.

"I want you inside," I whispered, brushing my lips gently

against his.

A low growl came from his throat, wild and untamed like the man I loved. Caleb released his grip on my hair and trailed his fingers down my side, making me shudder.

He found my clit and pinched the bud. I gasped, and he plunged his fingers into my tight, wet core again and again. I moaned in pleasure. Caleb withdrew his fingers and rubbed them against my lips. Another growl built in his chest, as I grasped them and pulled them into my mouth, sucking on my own juices.

He flipped me around, and the gaze in his eyes turned my body to molten fire. My heart pounded and all the air rushed out of my lungs.

"You are so fucking amazing. I love it when you taste yourself for me."

I leaned close so he could feel my breath on his ear when I replied. "I know," I said.

He growled, and a shudder racked my body. I needed him inside me. Now!

Caleb lifted me against the wall and teased at my entrance with his cock. I whimpered in anticipation and wrapped my legs around his body, willing him inside. He nudged in so fucking slowly, I thought I'd scream.

Caleb grinned. "Do you want me?" he asked.

"Fucking, yes."

"Tell me."

"I want you. Now fuck me, already."

Caleb flashed me that grin again but pushed in a little further. His massive girth stretched me, until, with one deep thrust, he entered all the way inside. I threw my head back and moaned.

"More," I demanded, and with each thrust, Caleb gave me what I wanted.

He captured my mouth with his and thrust his tongue inside as he thrust his cock deep into my core. His gaze locked with mine, and I saw the mischievous twinkle in his eye as he plunged into me over and over with every inch of his cock, slamming my bottom and back against the door as he fucked me.

I gasped for breath. His hips jerked. He growled again and pulled back, stilling his motion. He trailed sensual kisses down my neck as he walked me towards the bed. Lifting me high and off his cock, he pushed me down onto the mattress.

My heart thundered and a wave of excitement caused my stomach to flutter as Caleb stood watching me, studying me like I was the Dyna Wide Glide motorcycle his dad bought him for his eighteenth birthday all the way back in 2010.

But I studied him too. His perfect tattooed and muscular

body, his cock standing to attention. Both hard and taut and ready to pound into me.

A devilish smile played on his face. I trembled. He nudged his head between my thighs and flicked his thumb across the top of my clit as his fingers delved inside my wet and ready core. I groaned, and he replaced his thumb with his tongue, licking and sucking on my clit as he pumped his fingers in and out. His stubble from not shaving in the last few days bristled on my skin and sent shivers through my body.

He removed his fingers. I arched my back off the bed as he speared me with his tongue. His hand pushed my stomach down, holding me in place as he probed me relentlessly.

His strong hand smoothed up my body, over my hips and stomach, groping as it reached my breast. He swirled his fingertips across my nipple, before pinching it between his fingers and making my entire body quiver.

"I need you," I said, my voice barely audible above my panting breath.

Caleb moved his head from between my legs and sucked on my nipple like a man starved. He pinched one nipple between his fingers and nipped at the other, rolling his tongue around the taut bud. I couldn't breathe with the heat and intensity flooding through my body.

I grabbed his head and pushed him closer to my chest. Fuck, I wanted him. All day, all night, I couldn't get enough. We had four long years to make up for. Four dry years where neither of us had been with another person. I was going to take as much as I could for as fucking long as I could.

His rigid cock rubbed against my stomach, big and hard, making me gasp with need. I thought I might die if he didn't push inside me again, this second. As if reading my thoughts, he parted my thighs further and guided the head of his cock to my opening, slipping the tip inside and pulling it out again.

"Caleb," I murmured, "fuck me, now, please."

Caleb smiled and thrust forward. I arched my back and allowed him to fill me with the length of his shaft. I gasped as he pushed further in, and I wanted him to fill me completely.

His rock-hard chest quivered as I ran my fingers over it, tracing the lines of his tattoos. The pounding of his heart matched the beat of my own. He pinched my nipples as he thrust into me. Erotic pain pulled me closer and closer to climax. My body trembled beneath him, as he pulled my hips forward to meet his own and drove in harder and deeper.

"More." Sweat slicked my body and pleasure pulsed through me, building with each wave.

We moved in perfect unison. Intense sparks of energy enflamed my body and sent me careening over the edge. I pulled a pillow over my head to stifle a scream as the rush of my orgasm hit with an explosive force.

Unrelenting, Caleb withdrew his cock and sucked at my clit, trailing his tongue through my wet core.

"Oh, God," I moaned, not sure how much more I could take.

Caleb smiled and lifted his head for a second. I peeked at him from beneath my pillow.

"Shh," he said before pulling it away and throwing it across the room and sucking me in again.

It was too much. My clit throbbed, and wave after wave of pleasure pounded me as a second orgasm tumbled me into oblivion.

I could taste my arousal on his lips when he returned to kiss me. "I fucking love the look on your face when you come," he said.

"Then I think you'd better make sure to see it frequently." I said between gasping pants while I tried to recover my energy.

When I was finally sure my knees would hold me, I flipped Caleb onto his back and moved to lick the head of his cock. His fingers twisted in my hair, grasping tight. I trailed my tongue around his bulging edges and lapped at the pre-cum seeping from his head.

Caleb took in a sharp breath as I drew him deep into my mouth. I trailed my tongue around his smooth skin while sliding up and down his shaft with my lips. He gripped the blankets with both hands, his knuckles whitening from the pressure as he thrust forward, pushing deeper into my mouth. I eased back, teasing him.

"Amber." His voice came breathy with need. He tightened his grip on my hair and pushed me down. I smiled, drew him inside again, and watched his perfect face, even with the bruises that were some way from healing.

His eyes rolled back into his head. "Fuck, Amber. You're going to kill me," he growled, then flipped me onto my back. "Spread your legs and touch yourself," he demanded.

I chuckled and embraced the fluttery sensation in my stomach that came with Caleb's eyes watching my every move. I trailed my hand over my mound and found my clit. I circled it a few times, pinching it and rolling it between my fingers before parting my folds and pushing inside. Caleb growled, and his hand moved to his cock. His eyes filled with lust as he watched me play with myself.

My fingers moved slowly, teasing and stroking, delving in and out of my core. Caleb moved closer, kneeling between my legs. His fingers joined mine, teasing at my wet opening, as his other hand moved up and down his cock, pumping as he watched me.

My core clenched around his fingers, desperately wanting more. He grabbed my legs and pulled me forward, lifting one onto his shoulder and aiming his cock at my entrance.

"I missed you," he said as he drove himself home. His thrusts got faster and faster as he fucked me senseless.

The scent of my arousal filled the room. Caleb speared me over and over. He'd always been a great fuck, but now, there was something more. It was if we were joined anew. I'd been stupid to leave him, stupid to run away, but I sure would enjoy making up for lost time. I couldn't imagine my life without Caleb in it, and I knew he felt the same about me.

He pulled me onto his lap, thrust his hips upwards. And wrenched my head back before nuzzling my neck with his lips. Pleasure washed over me, and I couldn't contain the cry that escaped my lips.

"Fuck, Amber. I fucking missed you," Caleb said. "Come for me, again."

Caleb's expanding cock pulsated inside me. It quivered, and my core clenched, milking it for every last seed. Releasing together, we plunged into an all-consuming orgasm that caused me to scream, while Caleb muffled the sound with his hand, threw his head back, and grunted.

I wanted to cry with joy when he tumbled to the bed and lay beside me, his body and mine completely spent. I rolled onto my side and propped my head up on my arm.

"I missed you too," I said, and Caleb let out a full-blown

bellow of laughter.

"We have a lot of time to make up for." He kissed me deeply. "A very long time."

I rolled on top of him and propped my head on my arms. "I was thinking exactly the same thing," I said before nipping his bottom lip with my teeth.

EPILOGUE

(Two Days Later)

Amber

"You look good in a suit," I said and stood back to admire my man. "But you do not look comfortable."

"That's cuz I'm fucking not," he answered, and I knew the only reason I'd managed to get him into a suit in the first place was by saying Sophia had requested it. I knew he felt like we owed her for what Leo had put her and her family through, and he was right. The least we could do was look the part for her wedding day.

I sighed and looked around the room. The wedding had been perfect, and over in a flash. Sophia was dancing in her stunning lace fishtail gown. Ben was with her, looking for all the world like he was afraid of his two left feet.

I'd told Caleb that he'd be less conspicuous in a suit than he would in his leathers, but with the bruises displayed in full glory on his face, I don't think that was ever a possibility. Besides, the Landon brothers would stand out in a crowd no matter what they were wearing.

I smiled as he fidgeted. The man could walk unfazed into a gunfight but squirmed when forced to play dress-up. I smiled. He'd better get used to it, dress-up was one of Charlie's favorite games.

I watched her talking to Thea by the bar. Thea had been dragged there by Cane, who looked every bit as uncomfortable in his suit as Caleb did.

"Thank you for doing this," I said.

Caleb pulled me in for a side hug and smiled. So far, he'd resisted the temptation of surviving his ordeal by imbuing copious amounts of alcohol, but I wasn't sure how long that would last, especially now that Cane had caved.

I was about to suggest he have a drink if it would help him relax when he asked if I wanted to get some air for a few minutes on the balcony.

"Sure," I said and waved to Thea before signaling that Caleb and I were going outside. She was more than happy to keep Charlie with her.

The fresh air cleared my head and wiped the tiredness from my eyes. It had been a crazy few days, but I was happy to say things were settling down. We had a room in the hotel for the night but planned to drive to Denver in the morning and pick up mine and Charlie's things.

Caleb walked over to the balcony and looked out over the surrounding mountains. After the tumultuous weather that seemed to reflect events in my life, the sky had cleared, and bright sunshine had broken up the clouds for Sophia's big day.

Despite the earlier warmth, nighttime had seen the temperature drop, and when I stood next to Caleb, I shivered. He offered me his jacket and I accepted.

I raised my eyes to the sky. There were very few stars shining down on us, but a bright full moon bathed the landscape in a silvery sheen.

"It's good to be home," I said and put my hands in Caleb's jacket pockets. My right fingers instantly hit a small square-shaped box, and I pulled it out, holding it in my hands and gaping at it.

Caleb turned his head and looked at me before doing a double-take and snatching it from my grasp. "You weren't meant to see that yet," he said.

"What-what is it?"

A mischievous grin split his face, and he pulled me in for a tight hug. "It's a box."

I play-slapped him on the arm. "And what exactly is in the

box?" I asked.

"Something."

I swallowed, reached for the collar on his shirt, and pulled him down close to my lips. "What exactly would it take for you to tell me?" I asked and nipped his bottom lip.

"Fuck, woman! Is sex all you want me for?"

I tilted my head and pretended to think for a while. "No, it's not all I want you for. But it's definitely a bonus."

His lips met mine, and his tongue pushed inside. I moaned at the taste of him, and he clasped onto my bottom pulling me tight against his erection. My core pulsed as I imagined him thrusting inside me, teasing me with his cock the way he teased my mouth with his tongue.

I pulled back and wrapped my arms around his head. "You don't think I'm going to forget about the box that easily, do you?"

"No, but you're going to have to wait until after midnight before you see what's in it."

"And why's that exactly?"

Caleb moved his mouth close to my ear. "Because it's bad form to propose at someone else's wedding."

My breath hitched and my heart thundered. When I'd felt the box, of course, I'd wondered, but I hadn't really thought it was true. "When... when did you have time to get a ring?" I asked.

Caleb gave me a wry smile. "Four years ago. Just before Dad died. He helped me pick it out."

Another wave of regret washed over me. "I'm sorry," I said. "I ruined everything for all of us."

"No, you didn't." He looked down at me with a loving gaze. "I was thinking about this a lot last night. About all the regrets I had, and how I wished things could be different. But I realized how stupid they were. Leo lived his whole life looking back on his past. He couldn't let go, but we can. We can move on and not let our regrets define our future. We could wish to have spent the last four years together, but would you and Sophia be friends? Would Cane have gotten the chance to save Thea? I can't say for certain, but I don't think so. You became friends with Sophia because she was someone you could turn to who I would never suspect. Cane was only in the bar the night he met Thea because I was busy with the Feral Sons and Leo. If I had known about Leo four years ago, I would have fucking killed him then and there would have been no trouble with the Feral Sons." He huffed out a breath and smiled at me. "I'm fucking rambling and not making much sense," he said.

"No. It all makes perfect sense." I smiled. "No more regrets."

"No more regrets," he agreed. "We'd better get inside."

He moved to walk away, but I pulled him back. "What about Charlie?" I asked. "Will there really never be any regrets about not knowing if she's your biological daughter?"

Caleb smiled. "Never. For one, I believe she is. One look in her eyes tells me so. But even if that's not the case, she's still my daughter, and nothing will ever change that."

"No," I agreed. "Nothing will ever change that."

He looked down at me with a lust-filled gaze and smiled wickedly. "You know, we could get out of here. Sophia's too giddy to notice or care."

"What do you have in mind?" I asked.

"Well, I could ask Cane and Thea to look after Charlie for the night. We could go to our room and see how comfy the bed is?"

"I thought you wanted to stay up past midnight?"

"I have no intention of going to sleep."

I wrapped my arms around his neck again. "And there was me thinking I'd have to beg you to fuck me."

"Oh, you will."

~

Printed in Great Britain
by Amazon